The
Runaway
Robot

by LESTER DEL REY

Illustrated by Wayne Blickenstaff

SCHOLASTIC BOOK SERVICES

Published by Scholastic Book Services, a division
of Scholastic Magazines, Inc., New York, N. Y.

Copyright © 1965 by Lester del Rey. This Scholastic Book Services edition
is published by arrangement with The Westminster Press.

1st printing .... April 1966

Printed in the U.S.A.

Contents

1. Message from Earth

IT WAS AN EXCITING DAY. A rocket was due from Earth, and I guess nothing more exciting than that ever happens on Ganymede. Well, maybe when a manned spaceship comes in, it is more exciting, but a rocket is pretty important too.

The unmanned rockets brought supplies and messages from Earth and took back our herbs and fungi. These were very valuable because Ganymede is the only place in the System where they will grow. Therefore it is a vital satellite — not just another moon wheeling around Jupiter.

Actually you might say it is more important than Jupiter itself, because Jupiter does not produce anything of value to anyone. It hasn't even got a surface you can stand on.

Anyhow, the rocket was coming in, and Paul and I hiked over to the spaceport to see it.

The spaceport was about five miles from the residential domes, and Paul and I walked. We could have used Paul's skimmer, but we like to walk because you pass the caves on the way to the spaceport and the land is very rough there. It is too rough to skim low, and Paul's father, who is the governor of Sun Valley, forbids Paul to skim too high because it could be dangerous.

Paul is a boy, of course. He is sixteen years old and he has been on Ganymede with his mother and father and his younger sister, Jane, since he was three.

I am Rex, Paul's robot.

There are quite a few robots on Ganymede, over a hundred here in Sun Valley alone. Robots do all the work, so naturally there are many kinds. The ones here are farm robots. They are geared and activated to that kind of work. They plant and tend and harvest the herbs that we send to Earth. They scrape off the fungi that grow on the rocks, and process them for the juices that are valuable in Earth medicines.

I'm different, however. I'm a domestic robot, and therefore geared to a higher intelligence level than the others. I'm geared high enough to be a companion, and that was why Roger Simpson, Paul's father, bought me. I have been with Paul ever since he came here.

He was a toddler then, in a little air suit that made everybody laugh, and I could only take him on short trips out of residential domes. It was my job to watch him very closely and see to it that he did not take his helmet off or do some other foolish thing like that.

Later, when he grew up, Paul knew better of course.

Paul and I were very close, being together all the time,

and we talked about a lot of things. Once he tried to explain to me what it was like to grow up — to not know anything when you start and learn it all as you grow bigger.

It was very difficult to understand, because knowing things like the danger of a human going out without an air suit is built into a domestic robot's memory bank when it is manufactured.

Paul also taught me the big difference between a robot and a human — at least one of the big differences. Whenever Paul learned anything, he learned why it was true. I didn't. Like the air suit. Paul knew the reason why it was fatal to go without it or take it off. He learned all about air and how he needed it in his lungs to stay alive. I only knew it was dangerous, but I didn't know why.

And I guess maybe I still do not really understand it. Not the way Paul does at least. That is because my mental capacities are limited by my manufacturing specifications; and when you're born instead of manufactured, you have no mental limits.

A robot, I can tell you, gets a lot of wrong ideas. For instance, I thought I had curiosity. I got the idea from being with Paul and listening to him ask questions to find out about things. His mother called that curiosity.

I asked questions to find out about things, so I thought I had curiosity too. But I haven't. What I've got is this: *A limited capacity to inquire into unforeseeable conditions in order to avoid destruction.*

That was what it said in the instruction manual that came with me.

Not curiosity at all.

When Paul read that to me he laughed and said, "Don't worry, Rex. What you've got will do until some real curiosity comes along."

I have a "humor-response" circuit in my reaction bank, so I laughed too, but then I wondered what worry was — the thing Paul told me not to do. I asked him, and he said it was a crazy thing.

He said, "Don't worry about it." I didn't ask any more. But I did wonder how you could answer a question by saying the same thing over again that the question was asked about.

Anyhow, that was a very important day, and we started early to hike over and see the rocket come in; and when we came to the cave country, Paul said we had time to stop off and check our hide-out.

"Do you think someone might have found it?" I asked.

"Hardly. It's pretty well hidden, but there's always a chance. It's the near hide-out, remember."

By that he meant it would have been easier for someone to find than the far hide-out. We had two of them. The far hide-out was in the waste country on the Jupiter side of Sun Valley, about fifteen miles away.

Paul told me directions are always figured in relation to the mother planet, because Ganymede didn't revolve on its own axis. It went around the mother planet about once a week, but always with the same surface facing it.

This axis business was hard for me to understand, but I finally got it. Some satellites spin like tops, Paul said, and I wondered why they bothered to do that, but I didn't ask.

Stopping off at the hide-out turned out to be a good

thing because I had trouble, and it was lucky that it happened there.

Our hide-out is a cave in one of the jagged valleys in that area, and would be very hard for anyone to find because there are many of them. Paul marked ours by putting a very small sign at the mouth of the valley — a sign that read: HOLLYWOOD & VINE.

That is a place on Earth, Paul told me, a place he'd learned about from the entertainment tapes that come on the rockets. In fact, the name of the whole Ganymedian settlement that Paul's father governs — the plant, the farms, the residential domes, and the spaceport — is named Sun Valley, after another place on Earth.

Earth is the place all the humans on Ganymede want to go back to. Once I asked Paul what Earth was like, and he looked excited and said, "Like heaven, I guess." But I didn't know what heaven was either, so that didn't help much.

Over the cave, Paul had cut in very small letters: OPEN SESAME.

He got that out of one of his books, one that had *Fairy Tales* written on it. I don't know what fairy tales are.

A flat stone closed the cave tight. When we were inside, we could make it a vacuum by packing dirt around the edges, and we did this sometimes so Paul could use his portable air unit and take off his suit.

But we didn't do that on this particular day, because as soon as I got inside the cave I stopped and said, "Trouble."

This was our signal. When I said "trouble," it meant

something was wrong with me. Immediately, Paul began checking. In a minute, he said, "Oh, you've gone blind."

By word association, I knew what he meant. I'd blown out the refractor bulb in the front side of my control box, the box that stands on my torso box the way Paul's head stands on his shoulders.

It may seem funny to you, with your human brain, that I didn't know what was wrong with me, but that's how it is with a robot. I am not patterned to diagnose. I only know when I don't work right. Then it's up to the humans to find out what's wrong and fix it.

"Lucky we came to the cave," Paul said. "I've got some spare parts here." He unscrewed the faulty bulb and put in a new one.

He had tried to explain to me about seeing — what seeing is — but I never quite got it. He says that I have the capacity only for black and white, and that someday he'll get me a color refractor bulb. Then I'll see color.

That will be fine, except I don't know what color is. Paul tried to explain that too, but I don't understand it any better than when he told me that I see things two-dimensionally — everything on a flat surface.

Once, when he was a little boy, he said, "Rex, when I grow up and get rich, I'm going to have you repatterned up to the capacities of the computer robots."

They are the most advanced units ever invented, and it would be nice to be one, but I think Paul forgot that he was going to have that done. It is very natural for humans to forget. Robots can't. Everything goes into my memory bank and stays there. I couldn't forget anything even if I wanted to . . .

We left the cave after I'd been fixed, and hiked toward the spaceport. When we got close, Paul saw a skimmer coming from the direction of the plant.

"That's Dad," Paul said.

He would know that because his father's skimmer was red — that's a color — and was reserved for the governor. The skimmer stopped beside the rocket runway, and Roger Simpson got out and stood there waiting.

Paul and I didn't go any closer because he liked to watch the rocket come in from a little distance away.

"There it comes!" he shouted, and pointed high up into the sky. "It's beautiful."

I'd known it was coming for quite a while because my audio mechanism is far more sensitive than Paul's eyes and I could hear the jets hissing.

Paul grabbed me by the arm. His eyes were shining. "Isn't it beautiful? So long and sleek with its red jets flaming!"

The control robot in the tower was bringing the rocket in according to a punch-tape pattern. There were three lessening spirals, the rocket circling overhead. It stood out sharply against the sky and then vanished into the daytime blaze of Jupiter.

The last time around, it settled onto the rocket landing skid and the control robot braked it and killed its jets right where Paul's father and another man were waiting. The robot unlocked the rocket's loading ramp, and it opened and a ladder came out and touched ground. Mr. Simpson and the man climbed the ladder and disappeared into the rocket.

Paul dropped down and sat cross-legged as he stared at

7

the rocket. "They'll take out the supplies and fill it with Earth cargo," he said. "They'll launch it again, and it will travel a million miles an hour, straight and true, to its port of call on Earth. I'd like to be aboard."

"You'd die," I said.

Paul frowned. "Of course I'd die. There's no air in a rocket. I was speaking figuratively."

I said, "Oh, you mean you'd like to ride the rocket if it had air."

"Something like that," he replied impatiently, his attention on the rocket.

Paul got impatient with me once in a while, mainly when he was concentrating on something and I interrupted with stupid questions.

He did not look like his father. Roger Simpson was heavy-set and very robust and healthy-looking, very handsome by human standards. But Paul was somewhat thin in his body. They said this was because he'd grown up under the lower gravity on Ganymede. He was light-complexioned and had hair that was light brown, although I was never able to see the color. He had a thin, sensitive face that could change expression very rapidly. His face brightened up very suddenly when he got excited about something that pleased him.

And he got very excited now as his father came rapidly down the ladder from the hold of the rocket. Mr. Simpson was carrying a paper in his hand. He looked in our direction and waved it, calling, "Paul! Come over here. Come quickly! We've got to get home quickly! Your mother will want to hear the news!"

Paul sprang to his feet. "What news, Dad?"

Mr. Simpson didn't answer. He stood there reading the paper while Paul ran toward the rocket, and I ran along behind him trying to keep up.

I can run fast, but not as fast as Paul. If I try to run too fast, I fall down, which annoys Paul, for he has to stop and help me back on my feet.

I didn't get to the rocket as quickly as Paul, and when I got there, Paul was repeating his question.

"What news, Dad?"

But his father only smiled and made a playful pass at Paul's chin with his fist.

"Suppose we wait. We'll go home, and I'll break it to your mother and your sister and you all together. You wouldn't want to take unfair advantage of them, would you?"

I got the idea Paul wouldn't have minded at all. But he couldn't admit it.

"Come on," Mr. Simpson said. "Get into the skimmer and we'll head straight for the dome."

A robot crew, geared for unloading, was already marching double file toward the rocket ramp. They moved on a wide, caterpillar-type roller under their torso boxes. There was an endless chain studded by rubber cleats that took them anywhere they were sent.

"You too, Rex," Mr. Simpson said. "Into the skimmer."

That showed Mr. Simpson was in a happy mood, and I was glad because I liked riding in a skimmer. It was an open car with a flat bottom and three jets in the back end that lifted it off the ground and sent it skimming along a foot above the surface. A skimmer could be angled sharply upward and had the mechanical ability to function as a sky car, but such use could be dangerous. It was built primarily to skim the surface of the ground at high speeds.

We got home in no time. Mr. Simpson jumped out and Paul followed him, and I came along behind as usual.

The residential domes are not very big, only large enough to cover the entrances to the apartments and house. Living quarters for humans on Ganymede are always built underground. The air suits are left on the surface.

Paul and his father skinned off their air suits and rushed downstairs into the apartment. Mrs. Simpson and Jane were in the living room.

Mrs. Simpson was busy putting plastic strips on the weakened seams of an air suit. She looked up. "You look excited, Roger. What's happened?"

"We've been recalled. We're going back to Earth!" he told her.

There was dead silence. Paul, his eyes wide and unbelieving, whispered, "Dad, will you say that again?"

"Certainly, Paul. We've been recalled. We're returning to Earth."

2. Down the River

M RS. SIMPSON STARED at her husband, with a blank look
on her face, and he got the satisfaction of really
surprising his family. Then the hubbub started.

"Oh, Roger! When?" Mrs. Simpson jumped out of her
chair, and Mr. Simpson took her in his arms and swung
her around the way he often swung little nine-year-old
Jane.

It took quite a while for the excitement to die down.

I stood in the doorway without saying anything, and
after a while they quieted down. "How soon do we leave,
Daddy?" Jane asked.

"In about ten days," he said. "And that reminds me.
I've got some more news."

"Goodness," Mrs. Simpson laughed, "how *could* there
be any more than what you've told us?"

"There is," Paul's father answered, "and this is it. We aren't returning to Earth on any old passenger freighter."

This was amazing, and Paul stared at his father. "But, Dad, second-class ships are the only ones that make the Jupiter run!"

This was true. Anyone visiting the moons of Jupiter had to ride in the big, lumbering freighters that carried both pasengers and heavy supplies for the Moon colonies. This was because there was not enough luxury passenger trade that far out to make passenger runs possible.

Jane danced up and down, clapping her hands. "How are we going, Daddy? Tell us!"

"Well," Mr. Simpson replied, smiling, "this is going to be a big transfer of company personnel. They're sending an Orion-class space liner to pick us up. The *Star Queen*."

"Why, Dad!" Paul exclaimed, "they use Orion-type liners on the Venus runs. They have everything. Swimming pools, three-dimensional plays beamed in — "

"They even teleport fresh fruit — bananas, oranges," Jane added.

Mrs. Simpson patted her daughter's head. "You poor dear! You've never eaten a fresh orange, have you?"

Mr. Simpson laughed. "She hasn't exactly been starved. The frozen ones are pretty good."

"A luxury liner," Paul repeated as though he couldn't believe it.

He had told me all about how things are done in the inner planets — the big ships that take people to the resorts and vacation spots on Venus and Mars, the wonders of the Space Age that mean so much to humans.

"We've been pioneers for a long time," Mr. Simpson

said. "Now we're going back and learn to live like people again."

When Paul grabbed me by my arms and began dancing me in a circle, Mr. Simpson, who had quieted down, watched us very thoughtfully, with a slight frown on his face.

"Come on, Rex," Paul said. "We've got a lot to do and only ten days to do it in!"

He started to pull me out of the room, but Mr. Simpson said, "I've got an errand for Rex, Paul. I want him to take some papers over to the plant. While he's gone, I'll brief you on a few plans I have."

He spoke briskly, and though he wasn't sharp with Paul or anything like that, I could tell that something bothered him. Paul was too excited to notice.

"All right," he said. "I want to take as much of the load off your shoulders as I can, Dad."

Mr. Simpson smiled again — a kind of tight little smile I thought — and put his arm around Paul's shoulders. "Thanks, Paul. You're growing up now, you know, and you have to start facing some of the obligations of an adult — even the unpleasant ones."

I knew that meant something bad and I wondered what it was. Paul still didn't seem to notice. He said, "What's unpleasant about getting ready to go to Earth, Dad?"

Mr. Simpson didn't answer. He took an envelope from his pocket and handed it to me. "Give that to Mr. Kagen in the Number 2 refinery, Rex. You don't have to wait for an answer."

I left immediately, and on the way to the plant I did a

13

lot of wondering. Why had Mr. Simpson wanted to get rid of me? He had a reason. I was sure of that.

As I ran toward the plant, I thought about the ten days that would pass before the big luxury liner would take us back to Earth. And I was glad they were Earth days, not the longer ones based on Ganymede's revolutions around Jupiter. On Ganymede, a day and night is about a hundred and seventy hours long, compared to Earth's twenty-four-hour night and day.

Paul told me that on Earth the nights are very dark and the days are passed under the bright, blazing Sun. It's a little different on Ganymede. There it never gets very dark, because Jupiter fills most of the sky overhead and always reflects a lot of the Sun's light.

Ganymede goes by Earth time, with signals beamed out regularly from Earth to keep the chronometers right.

I reached the Number 2 plant without thinking of anything Mr. Simpson might have been upset about. Mr. Kagen, the foreman, was busy in his office, so I had to wait a while.

I passed the time watching a plant robot run a fungus-refining unit. You couldn't look inside, but I knew how it worked. The fungus was put in a tank at the top — big masses of it — and water was poured in. The water was heated, and that helped the fungus juices to run out when the pressure was applied.

The water and the juices were squeezed into a lower tank, and because the juices were heavier, the water always stayed on top. All they had to do was open a valve at the bottom and let the juice run into the shipment tanks. It was a very simple operation.

I stood there wondering what the juice did to heal people on Earth. I didn't really care — not right then. I was wondering a lot more about something else. When Mr. Kagen came out, I gave him the letter and headed right back to the residential domes.

I ran as fast as I could, but the trip took about an hour. When I let myself into the apartment, I heard Paul and his father talking.

They hadn't heard me come in, and I stopped where I was and listened, thinking that I'd be able to find out what the trouble was.

They were in the den with the door closed, and I couldn't get many of the words very clearly, but the voice tones showed that Paul was upset and angry.

This was unusual. Mr. Simpson wasn't the kind of parent that children argued with. I don't mean that he was harsh or cruel in any way. He and Mrs. Simpson believed in discipline — in their children doing the right thing — but they made it easy, because they were always more than fair and had their children's best interests at heart. Most of the time the Simpson home was full of laughter and gaiety. That was what made belonging to Paul so nice.

But now Paul was raising his voice to his father, and Mr. Simpson was being stern as a result. They moved closer to the door, and I heard some words.

Paul said, "It's not fair! Selling him down the river!"

Mr. Simpson laughed. "Where did you hear that expression?"

"I don't know. I heard it somewhere."

"You don't even know what it means."

I didn't know what it meant either. I knew what a river

15

was. Paul had told me they have them on Earth. Earth is almost all water and rivers where the water runs from one place to another. *Down* the river would mean with the current, because rivers respond to gravity and always follow the path of least resistance.

But I couldn't see what that had to do with whatever was bothering Paul. It was very mysterious, but I didn't want to get caught listening. I went to Paul's room and waited for him to come. I knew he would tell me all about it when he got there.

But he didn't.

He came into the room and saw me standing there and said, "Oh, it's you."

His tone was sullen, and he was frowning as he walked right past me and threw himself on the bed without paying any more attention to me. I didn't know what to say, not understanding his mood, so I waited.

This annoyed him. "Well," he demanded, "can't you say something? Do you have to just stand there?"

I knew it was very serious because he almost never talked to me that way.

"What do you want me to say?"

"Anything you feel like saying."

"It will be very exciting, going back to Earth."

"Yes, won't it!" He spoke the words sarcastically, and what I'd said seemed to make him even angrier. "What's so hot about Earth anyhow? Things haven't been bad on Ganymede."

"No, but on Earth you won't have to wear an air suit every time you go outside."

"I'll feel like a fool without my air suit!"

"No you won't, because other people won't be wearing them either."

"You're awfully logical for a robot," he snorted.

"I have a pre-established logic quotient that allows me to reason elementally."

"Oh, cut it out. I'm tired. I — I'm going to take a nap."

I stood there and waited while Paul turned over on the bed and scowled at me. A robot is supposed to be turned off when not in use. That's what happens to all the labor robots, because they run on batteries and it makes sense to save their charge.

But Paul had never turned me off. That was because I was a companion, and even after he went to bed we used to talk a lot. When he drifted off to sleep, I would stand and wait until he woke up and we'd go on from there.

A full charge lasted me about ten Earth days under those conditions, and when I got sleepy, it meant that my batteries were running down. When I went unconscious, they were empty.

The sullen look came into Paul's eyes as he got off the bed and reached for the switch box in my chest. I could hardly believe it.

I had never been turned off, but now I was going to be.

My last thought as he switched me off was to wonder what I'd done to make him angry . . .

I woke up. Mr. Simpson was in Paul's room with a stranger. Paul was not there.

As my consciousness came back, Mr. Simpson was say-

ing. "—one of Glenwood Electronic's best models. A
Q-5-7. This model turned out so well they're still manufacturing it. This one isn't self-repairing, but his intelligence level is only slightly below that of the computer
robots. He can read and write and do simple mathematics.
This of course conditions him for simple mechanical repair
work and even simple bookkeeping."

The stranger was a farmer. You could tell by his rough
hands, his worn leather clothing, and the squint of his
eyes from being out in the steady glare of the Ganymedian
Jupiter blaze.

"What language is it taped for?" he asked. He had a
heavy, gruff voice, and although you knew that he wasn't
harsh or cruel, he was all business.

"Only English," Mr. Simpson said, "but other language
tapes are available. I bought him as a companion for my
son, and he's been entirely satisfactory in every way. He
has a good personality."

I knew what was happening. I was being sold, and Mr.
Simpson was outlining my good points. That one about
personality was very important. Although robots are manufactured to exact specifications and all models should be
exactly alike, they are not. Robots have a personality leeway that gives each one a certain individuality within
its patterned capacities and limitations. Very few robots know such things about themselves. I know them because Paul and I talked about some of these things. I know
that some robots have certain sensibilities that are close
to being human. The activating structure in robots is very
complicated. When things go wrong with them, the built-

in safety factors are supposed to stop them in their tracks, but sometimes the factors do not work and a "sick" robot keeps right on functioning. Once in a while they go mad and become dangerous and have to be destroyed. A good personality is very important.

"I understand you're selling him because of shipping costs," the stranger said.

"That's right. A company rule excludes robots. They aren't on the Prepaid Personnel Relocation Lists. It will be cheaper to buy my son another robot when we get back to Earth — if he still feels that he wants one."

"He ought to find plenty of companionship on Earth," the stranger said, and I thought from the tone of his voice that he envied the Simpsons.

"That's what I'm banking on," Mr. Simpson said.

"What's your price?"

"I figured about five thousand."

"That's rather steep."

"He's a good robot. It would cost you more than that to bring in a simple laboring unit."

"All right. It's a deal."

I'd been conscious for quite a while, but I hadn't moved or said anything. Now Mr. Simpson said, "Rex, this is your new owner, Mr. Hennings. He has one of the biggest herb farms in the colony."

I said, "Hello, Mr. Hennings."

"Hello, Rex," he answered. "They tell me you have a pretty high intelligence level."

"Paul taught me a lot."

"Well, you won't have too much use for it — not for a

while at least. I'm buying you to work on the farm."

"Rex can supervise," Mr. Simpson said.

"I have an overseer for that, and two helpers. This will give me seven robots. I may buy another one later."

I was beginning to think that maybe Mr. Hennings was not as kind as I thought. But then he said, "The boy — does he know his robot's being sold?"

"Yes," Mr. Simpson said, "we talked it over."

"Maybe he ought to have a chance to say good-bye to Rex," Mr. Hennings suggested.

Mr. Simpson smiled. "If you've got a little time, I'd appreciate that. How about lunch before you start back?"

"I could do with a bite."

Mr. Simpson turned to me. "Paul is outside puttering with the skimmer, Rex. Why don't you go out and say good-bye to him?"

I did as I was ordered and found Paul sitting in the skimmer. He watched in silence as I approached him.

"Your father sent me to say good-bye."

"I suppose you think it's my fault — that this is my idea, selling you."

"No. It is your father's idea and it is very sensible. It would cost too much to take me back to Earth."

"It's mean!" he flared. "It isn't fair of them to take you away from me!"

"You are growing up, Paul. You won't need a companion much longer."

"Oh, quit sounding so noble."

"What is noble? That's a new word."

"Here we go again," Paul said. "Noble is — oh, forget

it. What good will words be to you, picking herbs and scraping fungus on a farm!"

"Mr. Hennings is a good man. He suggested we have a chance to say good-bye."

"You think I didn't want to say good-bye, don't you?"

"I think you feel bad, Paul. I think you're sad because you have to leave me here."

"Sure. But you don't see me doing anything about it, do you?"

"I think you would do something if you could."

He straightened up suddenly. "Get in."

"Why?"

He turned his head and stared at me. "That's the first time since we've known each other that you've questioned an order I gave you."

"That's true," I said. "I wonder why I did it."

"Because you aren't mine any more. You were wondering if Mr. Hennings would want you to get into the skimmer."

"Do you think that was the reason?"

"Yes. But get in anyhow. We'll go out to the cave."

I got in, and as Paul steered the speedy skimmer across the level surface of Ganymede, I wondered what his father would say. Would he be angry with Paul for taking me away?

It didn't really matter because we weren't gone very long. I looked forward to going to the hide-out again with Paul, but when we got there, it wasn't any good somehow. It wasn't the same. We didn't have anything to say to each other. We'd been in the cave only a few minutes when

21

Paul said, "Let's go back. I don't like this place any more."

We walked back to the skimmer and got back to the dome just as Mr. Simpson and my new owner came out.

I got into Mr. Hennings' skimmer with him, and after a quick good-bye to Jane and Mrs. Simpson, I rode away with him.

When I turned and looked back, they were waving, but Paul was not in sight.

3. Farmhand

THERE WERE THINGS I DIDN'T LIKE about my new life. I had no one to talk to. I was not allowed to read. I was turned off after each working shift, and my consciousness was not returned until it was time to go to work again.

But that didn't mean that I was treated badly by Mr. Hennings. Being kind to a robot is not the same process as being kind to a human being. Overworking a robot, for instance, is impossible as long as enough repair time is allocated (another big word Paul taught me). But a robot experiences sensations akin to human misery if he is made to work without proper repairs or to drag along on weak batteries.

Mr. Hennings insisted upon good care for his robots. His overseer, Mr. Bellows, was a grim, silent man who did practically no talking, but he was efficient and kept the robots in perfect shape, bringing them to full battery charge at the end of every third work period.

The work periods were geared to human capacity rather than that of the robots, because Mr. Hennings did not allow his mechanical units to function unattended. This may have been for reasons of greater production efficiency, but still it was humane. An unattended robot can damage one of its parts and have to stand motionless with the injury until help comes. It experiences a form of suffering, because a robot has a sense of self-preservation built into it, and with some badly adjusted units an injury to a part brings a kind of terror.

Mr. Hennings' six robots led what had to be called happy lives. Their construction is different from mine. Each of them consists of a single big rectangular box with two arms. These torso boxes are moved along on a broad, flat conveyor tread, revolving beneath them on an endless chain. This enables them to move efficiently between the row of growing herbs and go backward or forward as their guide mechanisms direct. They have long, tubular arms with sensitive steel-fingered hands, and when they gather herbs, they store and carry them in their torso boxes.

I am different. Built to work around humans and respond to more specialized orders, I have tubular legs and more flexible tubular arms. I also have a more specialized control box up above. There is a grill on either side of this box. These grills cover the diaphragms that serve me as both speakers and receivers, with short antennae above them to send or receive radio signals.

I have no nose or mouth, and only one eye, you might

say — the refractor bulb in the middle of my control box.

The overseer's two helpers were even more grimly silent than he was. They were native Martians and had the green, shell-like bodies that only Martians have.

I wouldn't have enjoyed talking to the Martians, but I thought Mr. Bellows might like a little conversation when he wasn't working.

I was disappointed. He preferred to sit by himself and read the newspaper and magazines that were taken on microwaves at Ganapolis, Ganymede's only city of any size, and distributed to the colonies all over the satellite.

After work the second day, I went to where he had his quarters, in a surface shed under the dome that covered the repair shops, and asked him if there was anything I could do for him.

He was a squat little Earthling with a deeply lined face and sharp bright eyes. He looked at me blankly and said, "Eh? What's that?"

"I asked if there is anything I can do for you."

"You did your work assignment."

"Yes, but I thought there might be something else. I can clean up your quarters."

He glanced suspiciously around. "They aren't dirty."

"I just thought I might help."

You could see that Mr. Bellows wasn't used to having things done for him. He said, "You were a houseboy over at the governor's, weren't you?"

"I was a companion for Paul, the governor's son."

"Well, I'm not a governor's son and I don't need a companion."

"We could talk after you get through reading. I am able to converse on many subjects."

"I don't want to talk! Especially not to a robot. It takes battery current, and that costs money. Have you been checked out?"

"No. I came straight to your apartment from the herb field."

"All right, get out there in the shed and get in line for your check-over. The boys don't want to wait all night."

"Yes, sir," I said. As I turned to leave I pointed to his table. "May I take one of those magazines to read tonight?"

He stared at me in popeyed amazement. "What in the galaxy is this? A robot asking for a magazine!"

You'd have thought I'd asked him for his head. "I'm sorry," I told him. "A magazine would help me pass the time pleasantly."

"You'll pass it pleasantly," he yelled. "You'll be turned off with the rest of the robots. Who do you think you are, a member of the royal Martian family or something? Get out of here!"

"Yes, sir," I said obediently and went out into the shed and lined up with the rest of the robots. I felt naked standing there as the two overseers checked the other robots over — naked because they had taken my pants away from me.

It probably sounds silly to you — a robot embarrassed without his pants. But domestic robots are given pants and aprons so that they can have pockets to carry small objects, and the first thing Mr. Hennings had said was that a farm robot wearing pants was ridiculous and he made me take mine off.

Everything considered, I wasn't very happy at Mr. Hennings' farm. I wasn't very happy standing there waiting to be checked out. They had taken my pants away, they wouldn't give me a magazine to read, and there was no one to talk to.

I was lonesome. That was the plain truth of it.

I was lonesome for Paul.

He had deserted me.

When that thought came, I took hold of myself quickly. It was no way to think. He hadn't deserted me at all. It was perfectly logical that I wouldn't be taken back to Earth by the Simpson family. After all, I was only a robot. I wasn't a human even if I did feel like one sometimes. At st I thought that what I felt must have been somewhat same as human emotions.

t that couldn't have been true. I had been built by to serve men and I could be destroyed by men. I had of the inalienable rights of human beings.

t I could miss Paul. And I did miss him. Right up to e second that one of the Martians checked me out and hen reached into my torso box and snapped me off for the night.

I kept right on missing Paul the next day and the next and the next. My work was mechanical and didn't take any concentration. All I had to think about were the things Paul and I used to do together: going to one of our caves to spend a lazy day talking about everything in the universe; riding across the country in Paul's skimmer, with Paul hanging on and Jane screaming with delight while I held her to keep her from falling off; spending the hours and the days and the years with Paul, watching him grow up, learning his moods — when he wanted to talk, when he wanted to be silent.

Missing Paul.

My torso wasn't big enough to carry herbs as an efficient operation, and I was assigned a specialized job. I was briefed on herb growth, and because the yields always ripened unevenly, I went around the farm and reported back on conditions in various areas so that Mr. Bellows knew where to send his six harvesting robots at just the right times. This was important because if the herbs got overripe, their values went down sharply at the processing plant.

This gave me quite a little freedom, and that was good. But then again maybe it was bad, because I was alone a lot, out by myself, and I thought more about Paul.

I had been on Mr. Hennings' farm about a week and wasn't rebellious. I was adjusted to my new service. I had no idea whatever of running away or anything like that. But one afternoon when I came in to report, Mr. Bellows had his radio going and I heard the announcer say:

"It's a beautiful sight indeed, the *Star Queen* coming down out of the sky into our spaceport. And a memorable occasion too, because this is the first time one of these proud ships of the inner planets has ever come to Jupiter. Her red and silver hull no doubt makes many of us here on Ganymede dream of home, and long for the day we too will return to Earth. We envy those who are going, but we are also happy for them — the ones who, two days hence, will board the mighty *Star Queen* and rocket down the spaceways toward the green hills of Earth . . ."

"What are you doing?"

"I've come to report."

It was Mr. Bellows scowling up at me from his planning board.

"All right, don't stand there. Give me your report and get back to work." He snapped off the radio. "Old windbag," he growled.

"You want to go back to Earth too, don't you?"

He glared at me. "Will you quit wasting current on idle chatter? What are the conditions in the south field?"

"Not quite ready, but most of that area is coming fast. I'll look again tomorrow. There are four patches in the southwest field that will be ready at noon tomorrow."

"How many robots?"

"Three."

"That's too many."

"Any less won't get the herbs picked in time."

"All right," he grumbled.

"I'm going to the east fields now."

"Well, get going. Stop wasting time."

I left the shed and trotted east, and I was thinking of what the announcer had said: *Two days hence . . . the ones who . . . will board the mighty* Star Queen . . .

That meant the Simpson family. It meant Paul.

And I knew I had to see him once more before he left.

It was a strange thought, and I suppose it scared me — a thought that involved disobedience, one that my discipline reactor should have destroyed instantly.

It tried. I was conscious of the struggle in my control box, but the thought remained whole. It was not destroyed. I had to see Paul once more before he left for Earth, and there was only one way to do it.

I was going to run away.

I would not become a renegade robot. I would come back after the *Star Queen* cleared Ganymede.

But when the Simpson family boarded her, I was going to be somewhere in the crowd where I could get a last look at Paul.

4. Runaway

WHEN MY POWER WAS TURNED ON the next morning, nothing had changed. The thought was still there. I was going to run away.

It didn't frighten me any more. Now that it was an established idea, my thought processes took over and used it as a base for planning.

I decided to leave the next morning. I would start off in the direction of the spaceport on my first checking assignment and keep right on going. My specifications allow me to run safely at a speed of about eighteen miles an hour, and I can maintain that pace indefinitely. Running takes quite a little power, however, and even with a full charge, the four-hour run to the spaceport would eat up power that would last through an ordinary day. But that would still leave me ample power to return to Mr. Hennings' farm after the *Star Queen* blasted off.

I was a little sad about what would happen after I got back. If Mr. Hennings thought I'd lost orientation and wandered away, it would make me unreliable and he would probably put a governor on me. That's an electronic mechanism which overrides a robot's self-control and makes it impossible for him to go beyond a preset perimeter. A governor would make me a prisoner.

I didn't care about that. After Paul left for Earth, Mr. Hennings' farm would be as good a place as any for me to stay.

Luckily, we were all recharged that night, and the next morning when I started out I was full of energy. I reached Mr. Hennings' portside boundary and looked back. There was no one in sight, so I kept going.

I set my pace at safe capacity and jogged off toward the spaceport.

As I traveled, I saw several skimmers move here and there in various directions, but none came very close to me. It wouldn't have mattered anyhow, because they would think I was running an errand for my owner.

Nor would anyone recognize me as the robot that Mr. Simpson had sold to Mr. Hennings. I was different from the farm robots, but there were quite a few of my type and model on Ganymede. The only positive identification I had was my serial number. All robots have serial numbers cut into plates riveted to their torso boxes in front. But a serial number never means anything to anyone unless that particular robot has been stolen or has gone voluntarily out of bounds.

I jogged comfortably along, the miles vanishing under my aluminum feet, and in about four hours the spaceport reared up on the horizon. A little farther on I could see the *Star Queen* standing proudly in her berth.

She was so big she made everything around her look small by comparison. Even the control tower, the highest point at the spaceport, reached only halfway up her hull.

As I came closer, I could see the people looking very small around the great ship. A big crowd had come from many miles to see the *Star Queen*.

There was a great deal of bustle and activity. Two freight ports were open, and a force of robots was loading the belongings of the families that were being relocated back to Earth. There was a lot of furniture, a lot of crated objects. A thought occurred to me — it didn't seem that one five-foot robot would have made much difference.

But that was feeling sorry for myself. I killed the thought and moved quietly into the crowd. Nobody paid any attention to me. There were quite a few robots in the area, some waiting for their owners; others, given more personal freedom, were walking around enjoying the spectacle.

I circled the ship, looking at it from all sides. Most of the activity was on the loading side, with the freight ports rearward and the passenger ramp up front.

There was a big carpet at the foot of the passenger ramp and a lot of people dressed in their very best, milling around, talking and laughing — the people who were going and the ones who were bidding them good-bye. I pushed through the crowd in the opposite direction.

But then I froze, scared — scared clear through. A skimmer stopped at the far forward end of the ship and

33

two men got out, Mr. Hennings and Mr. Bellows. They were both scowling, and it was easy to see that they were there on business.

They were looking for a runaway robot.

I didn't stop to wonder what had gone wrong. That didn't matter. My mental energy was needed for more important things — things such as how to avoid being caught until I'd seen Paul get aboard the *Star Queen*. That was what I had come for and that was what I intended to do: get one last look at Paul.

After that, I didn't care much what happened to me.

I looked around and saw three domestic robots of my type standing in a group. They were talking to each other and looking up at the ship.

I moved in that direction and sidled up behind them. That way, if Mr. Bellows' darting eyes spotted me, identification would be almost impossible.

But the three robots soon moved off in separate directions. I followed the one walking away from the ship, hoping my owner and his overseer would look in the other direction.

Then I got another fright. A worse one. I had forgotten about my pants. I didn't have any pants on, and the other robots wore pants and aprons.

Luckily, I was near a pile of empty crates, and I ducked behind it just as Mr. Bellows' eyes swung in my direction. I was pretty sure he hadn't seen me, but I couldn't be absolutely certain until I went to the far side of the pile and peered out. The two men had not moved from the place where I'd last seen them. They were standing beside the big carpet by the passenger ramp. Mr. Bellows was

34

scanning the crowd, and they seemed to be waiting for someone.

Something buzzed in my control box. I gripped a side of an empty crate in my steel hand, and it broke into splinters. The Simpson family had arrived at the passenger ramp and were getting out of a skimmer.

They were all there, the four of them, but my whole attention was on Paul. And I could see that he wasn't very happy. Not like Jane, who was laughing and pulling at her mother's arm as she asked questions. Nor like his father, who was being very adult, but couldn't hide the pleasure that glowed in his face.

Paul was not smiling. He looked broodingly at the big ship, as though he didn't care whether it was there or not. His eyes scanned the crowd restlessly.

He took no interest in anything around him until Mr. Hennings saw the Simpsons and ran toward them, with Mr. Bellows following him. Mr. Hennings was angry and he waved his arms as he talked.

I tried to follow his lips to see what he was saying, but I didn't have to. I knew what he was saying. And I knew what had gone wrong. I had been missed at the farm. They'd probably been watching me even more closely than usual, and when I couldn't be found they assumed I'd run away and gone back to Paul.

It had been the logical thing for them to think, and I'd been stupid not to realize it. But none of that mattered, really. I had achieved my purpose. I was safely hidden in a place where I could watch Paul and his family board the *Star Queen*.

Mr. Hennings was angry, and I didn't have to hear his

words to know what he was saying. He asked if I had gone
back to the Simpsons', but Mr. Simpson shook his head,
genuinely surprised at my having run away.

Mr. Hennings said something more, and Mr. Simpson
turned to Paul and asked a question. Paul shrugged and
shook his head also. He didn't look unhappy about my
escape, but not as obviously overjoyed as Jane. She made
no effort to hide her happiness until Mr. Hennings frowned
at her, and her mother bent down and told her to be quiet.

Mr. Hennings and Mr. Simpson had further conversation
on the subject of my escape. I don't know whether Mr.
Hennings asked for his money back or not. Probably not,
because the sale was legal and delivery had been made.

He was obviously disappointed at not finding me with
the Simpsons or at least hanging around in their vicinity.
He conversed with Mr. Bellows for a few moments and
then both men moved back and stood watching the ship.

The passengers were boarding now, and my escape
was a closed subject as far as the Simpsons were concerned. After all, it wasn't their problem and they had
more important things to think about. They were going
back to the green hills of Earth.

Paul's whole manner had changed. He'd brightened
and become more alert. His eyes were darting here and
there, searching the crowd, and I was tempted to run out
and wave to him, so that we could say a final good-bye
before he boarded the ship.

I might have done it too, but he turned abruptly and
hurried up the ramp and disappeared into the *Star Queen.*
I watched as the rest of the Simpson family followed

him, waving to their friends until they too disappeared into the port.

It was over. I felt let down. There was nothing holding me now, no reason not to walk out from behind my shelter and give myself up.

I didn't dread it particularly. I knew Mr. Hennings would put a governor on me. A proved runaway, he would be foolish not to, because for a robot second chances are unheard of. Anything a robot does once, he will usually do again, unless what he does is caused by a breakdown. And what I'd done hadn't been for that reason.

I didn't dread the punishment I would receive. But I didn't rush out to give myself up. Mr. Hennings and Mr. Bellows had not moved. They stayed where they were, watching the passenger ramp being dropped from the ship. It was pulled away and the port was closed as the people down below gave a final cheer.

The loading had been finished, and the cranes were starting to move away from the freight ports. I glanced in that direction and something caught my eye.

There was a rope hanging from the rear port, and as I watched, a figure appeared in the port. It moved swiftly and with decision, grasping the rope and leaping out toward the ground.

It was a human, a boy, escaping from the ship.

It was Paul.

I stared, strange new emotions banging around in my control box as he came swiftly down the taut rope, reached the ground and ran toward the freight yard several hundred feet away.

My controls questioned what my refractor tube claimed to have seen, but there was no doubt about it. The boy had been Paul.

It may seem strange to you that his escape didn't cause a lot of excitement, but there was no reason why it should have. Nobody was paying any attention to the freight ports. The robots Paul encountered couldn't have cared less what he did. They were not conditioned to stop escaping boys. Nor did the foreman in charge of the loading take the escape seriously. They couldn't imagine a legitimate passenger on an Earth-bound ship wanting to get off. They probably thought Paul was a local youth who had sneaked onto the *Star Queen* for a thrill and was getting off the best way he could.

At the time, Paul's escape was important to me only. I smashed a heavy box to splinters in my excitement. I wanted to run to him, but that would have been foolish. Everything was changed now. I had no intention of giving myself up. Hennings' stupid farm was the last place in the universe I wanted to be. Paul had left the *Star Queen* and I wanted to be with him.

At that precise moment Mr. Bellows and Mr. Hennings went into action. The crowd had been pushed back from the *Star Queen*, and she was moving as the powerful underramp hydraulics pushed her slowly toward the blasting pits.

The ship had moved. That meant that Paul was not going to be aboard when she blasted away. Even if the authorities discovered him, it was too late. The blast-off cycle had been started and would not be stopped for anyone or anything.

The crowd was still watching the ship, but Mr. Hennings and his overseer, after a few moments of conversation, began moving in my direction. They had decided to search the area.

I looked around for cover. There were quite a few obstacles scattered around the port — things I could hide behind — but reaching them unobserved was the problem. I backed away, keeping the pile of boxes between me and the two men, and when they reached it I had found a tool shed to hide behind.

They searched the pile and then debated their next move. If they had split up, I would have been lost. But as it was, they stayed together, and when they moved to the left I used the tool shed as a cover and backed away again.

Dodging them in this manner, I reached some rocks on the far edge of the spaceport and found safety just as the *Star Queen* blasted off. Everyone, including myself, stopped to watch. It was a magnificent sight, a demonstration of applied power such as Ganymede seldom saw — suddenly expanding gases hurling tons and tons of metal out into space, out past the gravity pull of Jupiter, high into the free fall of the void.

And even more miraculous was the technology that had solved space and motion problems to a point where not a single passenger received any of the shock quotient involved.

I had been given the mentality to marvel at this, but I had no time to dwell on it very long. I had to keep track of my two pursuers.

They seemed to have lost their enthusiasm for the hunt

by now, and as I watched from behind a rock they turned away from the ridges and went back to their skimmer. For the time being, they had given up.

As soon as they were out of sight, I ran to the freight yard. I searched it from one end to the other, but I didn't find Paul.

He hadn't taken any chances on a search. He had used the *Star Queen*'s blast-off to make his own escape.

But I thought I knew where to find him: in one of our hide-outs. My only problem was to guess which one. I didn't have much to go on. It would only be a guess. But I chose the far one because we usually kept more supplies hidden there.

I took a last look around the freight yard and headed in that direction.

5. Robot Hunt

I T WAS A FIFTEEN-MILE JOG to the far hide-out, and while
running doesn't tire a robot, I was still bothered by the
uncertainty. Would Paul be there?

Then, too, when you're doing something like running
which doesn't take brainpower, a lot of thoughts can creep
into your mind. With me, it was doubt. Had the boy I'd
seen sliding down the rope from the freight port of the
Star Queen really been Paul? What if my senses had
deceived me? After all, I was only a robot, not a human.
It would be terrible, after having my hopes built up, not
to find Paul at the hide-out.

And there were other thoughts too. The question I had
asked Paul about: What was worry? What did fear
feel like, and how did a human know when his mind was
troubled?

41

I was beginning to understand. Synthetic or not, I was experiencing emotional reactions that, as Paul had put it, might not be genuine but would do until real ones came along.

Another thing. After I had seen Paul get off the ship, after the promise of seeing him again, the thought of going back to Hennings' farm caused great agitation in my control box. The farm was no longer as good as any other place. It was the worst possible place to be. I did not want to go back.

That thought brought another — the memory of something I'd once heard Mr. Simpson say. He'd been talking to Paul about something, and I had heard only these few words which Mr. Simpson spoke: *After a taste of freedom, captivity is no longer the same.*

It had meant nothing to me at the time, but coming out of my memory bank, there was meaning attached to it. I'd had a taste of freedom, and captivity on Mr. Hennings' farm would no longer be the same.

But I would go back of course.

Or would I?

I soon forgot all about Hennings and his miserable farm because I was approaching the far hide-out and my diaphragms were straining for a sound of someone inside.

But there wasn't any sound. Everything was as quiet as the places called cemeteries, where humans bury people after they die.

I lifted the stone away from the entrance and went inside. It was empty and quiet and lonely.

I had guessed wrong. Paul had gone to the near hide-out. That meant another jog of over twenty miles. But then suppose I didn't find him there either? Suppose I *had* been mistaken about seeing him leave the *Star Queen?* Could I go back to Hennings' farm without knowing for sure?

That was unthinkable — to wonder for the rest of my life.

But suppose I didn't go back. What then? My charge had been full, but it was running out. In a matter of a few days I would begin to get hungry. Not the same hunger humans feel, but still a signal that my batteries needed fresh nourishment. Before oblivion, I would get very tired.

Oblivion! Without knowing what had happened to Paul! Again, it was unthinkable. I would have to conserve my energy, make it last. I couldn't turn it off because I wasn't equipped with a timer.

Suddenly none of that mattered any more because I heard a voice.

"You're getting pretty careless, aren't you?"

"Paul!"

"I could have walked up and unscrewed your serial plate. What happened to your ears?"

I almost fell down turning around, and then I saw him standing in the cave entrance. I stood there not knowing what to do or say. I felt like jumping on him, grabbing him, but of course I couldn't do that. A steel robot doesn't go around grabbing humans. They are made of flesh that tears and bones that break.

"You were so quiet," I said.

"You should have been able to hear me breathe."

"There must have been some static in my receiver."

"You're probably getting old," he grinned. Then his face straightened and he looked very stern, and I saw for the first time that he resembled his father a great deal.

"What are you doing out here?" he demanded.

"I was looking for you."

"But you're supposed to be picking herbs on Hennings' farm. What have you got to say about that?"

"I ran away."

"You ran away! You mean you're a renegade robot?"

"I guess so."

"That means it's my moral duty to report you." He scowled at me and stood with his shoulders very straight. "Come here and let me disconnect your batteries."

I took two obedient steps forward, and suddenly Paul couldn't act any longer. He burst out laughing and threw himself on me and began pounding my torso box with his fists.

"Oh, Rex! I'm so glad to see you, I could kick a hole right through Jupiter!"

All my controls were rattling from his fists beating my sheet-metal sides, but I didn't care. I was full of some crazy emotion and I was mad at myself for not being able to express it. I could only stand there like a big lump of iron.

"You should sit down and rest," I said. "You must have run all the way out here."

"Don't worry about me," Paul replied. "You're the one

44

to worry about. How much of a charge have you got left?"

"It's hard to estimate. I've been running a lot and I've been putting a strain on it. But I'm not hungry yet."

"You're the one who'd better sit down." He scowled again. "Maybe I'd better turn you off while I think."

"Don't do that. I wouldn't be able to help you."

"Help me! Are you telling me I need a robot to help me think?"

He laughed again, and dropping to the ground, sat with his back against a rock. I could tell he was tired, but of course he would never have admitted it.

I squatted down too. "Why did you leave the *Star Queen*, Paul?"

He tried to look disgusted and did a very good job of it. "That old tub? One look at the inside and I didn't want any part of it. I'd have been bored stiff limping back to Earth in that pile of junk."

I knew he did not expect me to believe any of that. He was evading, the way humans do when they're embarrassed. His actions had been more sincere than his words, and spoke much louder.

"Your parents must feel pretty bad," I said.

He frowned. "I'm not a child any more. They don't have to worry about me."

"They will, anyway."

"The important thing is what we're going to do now."

I could have told him that. We were going to wander around a while, and then he would board the next ship out of Ganymede headed for Earth. After he was gone I would return to Hennings' farm.

This was all that could happen. Wherever we went on Ganymede, all roads would lead to that destiny for both of us. It couldn't be any other way.

"You asked about my power," I said. "What about yours?"

He looked down at the power in his air suit. It was attached just above the belt, and it renewed the air that flowed into his plastic helmet.

"It's in good shape. Besides, I can pick up a fresh pack without any trouble."

"Where?"

He started to answer. Then he stopped to think, and I outlined the difficulties.

"They'll find you missing on the *Star Queen* and radio back. That will alert the whole satellite, and they'll be watching out for you. They'll probably even start an active hunt."

"You're right," he said.

You didn't have to be very smart to figure that out, but the rest was more difficult. Paul would need power and food.

"Have you had anything to eat?"

"No. I was too excited to get hungry."

I pointed to the supply packet inside his suit on the side opposite the power pack. All suits have them — places for emergency rations.

He glanced down, his face blank. "It's empty. I for-

46

got to fill it. As a matter of fact, I didn't have time."

"We've got some dry stuff in the cave."

We went inside, and after sealing the entrance, turned on the portable air unit. As soon as Paul could breathe, he took off his helmet and we checked our supplies by the light of the Croydon ray unit we kept there.

"Not much," Paul said ruefully. "We should have been more careful about keeping the place stocked up."

There was a small box of cookies and some dried bread.

"You'd better eat what's here," I said.

"No. I'll only eat a little. It's got to be rationed."

But it didn't work out that way. We decided the best thing to do was to try to get back to the Simpson apartment in the residential section, and that it would be better to travel after dark. That meant a wait of some four Earth hours.

I suggested that Paul get some sleep while we were waiting, and he dozed off and took short naps.

But when we were ready to go, the food had been nibbled away until there was none left.

The only real trouble we feared was being seen and stopped by those who were probably out hunting for Paul already. If we reached the apartment safely, there would be no problem about supplies.

At least that was the way we figured it, but again it didn't work out that way.

We traveled slowly to conserve my power. I kept waiting for hunger to set in, but it didn't, and we made the trip to the edge of the residential section safely.

At that point we became extremely careful, because there could be activity, and the Ganymedian darkness is not very deep. The glow of Jupiter, even at night, eternally fills the sky.

We crept through the domes, using all the cover available, and when we reached the Simpson apartment I adjusted my diaphragms to the peak of efficiency and listened with one mechanical ear against the wall.

"There is no one inside," I said.

We entered the dome and hurried down the stairs, familiar with our surroundings, and Paul waited until I'd closed the door before turning on the light.

He snapped the switch, and we found — nothing.

It was quite a shock. The apartment was empty. We rushed around looking in cupboards and closets, and returned to the living room.

"They moved mighty fast; I'll say that for them," Paul exclaimed.

"Thieves and vandals," I said.

Paul shook his head. "No. Dad gave several families permission to scavenge the place after we took out the things that went on the *Star Queen*. But I didn't think they'd come in so fast."

"After all," I said, "your father was the governor. Your family had nice things."

"I wish they hadn't been quite so nice," he answered. "What do we do now?"

"Let's go over it again. We might have missed something."

We gave the place another going-over, and this time
Paul came back with something the scavengers had missed:
a small helmet radio. "It was back on a shelf in my
room. It's in good working order."

Helmet radios were a convenience, but not many
people on Ganymede used them because they took up
precious space in a helmet and were annoying.

Paul said, "I guess this is about all —"

I cut in sharply. "People coming! We've got to get out
of here!"

We just made it, melting into the shadows behind one
of the domes as a party approached the Simpson apartment and entered.

Paul grinned. "Are they going to be disappointed!"

"Not if they catch us," I said. "Let's get going."

We moved clear of the residential section and decided
to go to the near hide-out. It seemed to be the only place.
I was beginning to worry about my power pack. I still
had power, but I was getting faintly hungry, and a fresh
supply was nowhere in sight.

I was trying to think of a solution when Paul stopped
dead in his tracks and stared at me.

"What's the matter?"

He looked blankly at the radio he held in his hand. "I
was listening," he said.

"What did you hear?"

"A newscast. They say that you kidnaped me off the
Star Queen. That means they think you've gone mad,
Rex."

49

A mad robot. It happened sometimes, and there were very strict laws as to how to proceed in such cases. I stared silently at Paul, and finally he said it.

"That means you're to be destroyed on sight — no questions asked."

I'd seen that happen once. A quick blast from a ray gun with all inquiries made afterward. Paul's protests could not help me, because strange powers sometimes develop in the reactors and coils of a mad robot — deadly hypnotic powers.

"We've got to separate," I said. "You've got to go straight to the airport and tell them who you are. I'll go back to Hennings' farm and see what happens. Mr. Hennings paid a lot of money for me. Maybe he'll think twice before he —"

"Rex!"

"Yes?"

I turned to look at him. He had straightened up, and his face was grim. He looked even more like his father as he said, "I didn't jump ship and give up a trip to Earth because I wanted to stick around and admire the Ganymedian landscape. I did it because I refused to leave without my robot. I disobeyed my father because — well, I did what I did, and I'm not going to run back to the spaceport like a whipped pup. We stay together. Is that understood?"

Paul was a human. I was a robot. There was only one thing I could say, no matter how I felt.

"That is understood."

50

"O.K. We'll take it right from here. We'll go to the hide-out and make plans."

I'll admit I was a little nervous. Things had changed. If we were seen, no one would rush up and grab me. They would stalk me very carefully.

At any moment a ray gun might blast out and turn my control box into a puddle of molten metal.

An uncomfortable thought . . .

6. Hide-out

SAFE IN THE NEAR HIDE-OUT with the door sealed, Paul refreshed himself with a long drink of water from the supply tank he kept there. Also, we were a little luckier in the food department — three packages of cookies and a whole loaf of bread with a piece of hard cheese.

Paul feasted. He was so hungry that he forgot to ration the food and had reduced it by half when I took what was left of the bread and put it back.

"That solved one problem," he said. "Let's go on to the next one."

"Which one shall we start with?"

"Let's skip momentary things and look to our long-range objectives."

"What are they?" I asked.

"To get off Ganymede."

"That's a real objective all right. How shall we go about it?"

"Any suggestions?"

"The thought of a spaceship presents itself."

Paul blinked. "You're really learning to express yourself, Rex."

"I've had a good teacher."

He didn't say anything, but he patted my steel arm affectionately and his eyes again turned thoughtful.

"Maybe we're thinking too far ahead."

"That's a possibility."

"Our major problem is your power. We've got to give some thought to that."

"I've been thinking about it pretty steadily."

"Any ideas?"

"I think you ought to turn me off." He frowned, and while he was pondering the suggestion, I continued. "It seems to me it might be wise to stay here a while. The report of my kidnaping you should start some hunts. But I don't think they'll explore the caves because they wouldn't expect a mad robot to hide."

This was logical because the pattern of robots gone wrong was usually different. Fear and caution were hardly ever a part of a mad robot's pattern. They usually stayed out in the open and dared anything.

"That makes sense," Paul said.

"As far as turning me off is concerned, you're going to have to sleep yourself. There's no point in my staying conscious."

"How long do you think we should stay here?"

"About three days. The hunting parties should get discouraged by that time."

"Uh-huh. Three days of roaming around with no results, and they'll start believing other rumors — that I didn't get off the ship, that I'm hiding somewhere on the *Star Queen*, that you broke down and fell in a crevasse somewhere."

"Three days, then?"

"It's settled."

"All right. Why don't you turn me off and get some sleep? We can make more plans later when you're rested."

Paul yawned. "Another good idea," he mumbled. "Things have been moving pretty fast."

He opened the door under my serial-number plate and grinned. "See you in the morning," he said, and snapped the switch.

The power that activates a robot is of extremely high potency. All its habit channels have never been charted thoroughly, and it is believed that a latent residue remains active and uncontrolled for a few microseconds after they disconnect. This can cause a robot to have dreams.

I had one.

I dreamed that I was walking along and that a human reared into view from behind a ridge. He had a ray gun. He yelled, "Mad robot! Mad robot!" and fired the gun. And my control box turned into a steaming cinder . . .

"Wake up, Rex."

54

My refractor bulb went on, and I saw Paul yawning and stretching.

"How long did we sleep?" I asked.

He looked at the chronometer on his wrist. "Holy smoke! Twelve hours. I'm starved."

"Careful with the food. It's got to last."

He opened a box of cookies. "It's all right. When we get out of here, we'll get some more."

"Where?"

"I think we ought to go to Ganapolis."

"How will we get there?"

While we were talking I was listening to sounds outside the cave. Several humans were walking very quietly out there — so quietly that Paul couldn't hear them.

They made an awful racket on my diaphragms, however, and I measured their approach toward the mouth of our cave. I didn't say anything to Paul because I didn't see any point in making him nervous unless it was absolutely necessary. And I was glad I had kept quiet because the party went right on by. Luckily for us, they weren't very observant in the Ganymedian dusk.

But it proved the wisdom of our holing up in the cave. There were probably quite a few hunting parties out looking for the mad robot. They were, of course, all public-spirited citizens with the interests of the community in mind. But there was also a standing government reward for destroying a public menace. That might have helped a little too.

"A skimmer," Paul was saying.

"Where will we get a skimmer?"

"I sold mine to a man who lived near us. I can borrow it back. When they find it in Ganapolis, they'll return it to him. It's registered."

"That would be stealing, wouldn't it?"

"Not if I paid."

"Then he'd know who you are. I still think that would be stealing."

Paul scowled. "You're doing an awful lot of thinking lately," he grumbled.

"Your father and mother wouldn't like it."

It bothered Paul too, but he didn't want to admit it. "Doesn't self-preservation count for anything?"

"Are you sure it's a good idea to go to Ganapolis?"

"It's the only place we've got a chance of buying food and getting you a charge."

He was right about that. Ganapolis, a hundred miles away, was the closest city where there were stores and restaurants and all the things that make up a city. Sun Valley, the colony that Roger Simpson had governed, was in the outlands, with one supply depot, where Paul wouldn't dare show his face. The Ganapolis spaceport was far bigger than that of Sun Valley, and the *Star Queen* had come to the colony only because moving all the freight to Ganapolis would have been too difficult. It was easier to install a special jetting device at the Sun Valley spaceport.

"Let's face facts, Rex. You haven't got enough charge to walk to Ganapolis. Yet it's the only place we can go. We've got to have a skimmer. And I say paying for what you use isn't stealing."

"There's something else we could do."

"What?"

"You could go to the Sun Valley spaceport and give yourself up. Then you might be able to convince them I'm not mad. They'd send you home, and I'd go back to Mr. Hennings."

"That's out," Paul said firmly. "They might think I'm under your influence and destroy you anyhow. But even if they didn't, it's out."

I was a robot. Paul was a human being. He had given an order. My suggestion was out.

"Incidentally," he said with anger, "I'm not stealing you from Mr. Hennings. I don't think Dad had any right to sell you in the first place, because you were my robot. He gave you to me. Besides, when things quiet down I'm going to reimburse him."

"What are you going to use for money?"

"Dad gave me the money he got from Mr. Hennings, and I have some of my own."

I hadn't known that. I thought the whole thing over and decided a robot wasn't equipped to struggle with human problems of morality. What Paul said seemed logical. It was difficult to see how you were stealing something you paid for.

But the skimmer business seemed different — until I thought of something else.

"I'll steal the skimmer and leave the money," I said.

"Why you?"

"Because I'm a robot, and robots do not have souls. If I'm dishonest it doesn't make any difference."

And Paul fell back on the old saying he used so often. His eyes softened, and he put his hand on my arm. "Maybe not," he said, "but what you've got will do until a real soul comes along."

He was wrong, of course. I'm nothing but a superbly controlled and directed supersonic wavelength. But he made me feel good all the same.

"Besides," I said, "I'm the logical one to get the skimmer. You would be recognized. You wouldn't have a chance if anyone recognized you."

"What about you?"

"They're looking for a mad robot, and I won't act like one. Also, they're looking for a robot with a kidnaped boy under his arm, and I'll be alone. I doubt if they're questioning every robot that's going about its peaceful business."

"But the thing to do is not be seen."

"I'll try not to."

We decided to use this plan: after our three-day hiding period was over, I would go and get the skimmer and leave the money and we would try to reach Ganapolis.

With all the decisions made and nothing to think about, things got pretty dull there in the cave. We fussed around, doing not much of anything, until Paul was sleepy again. Then he turned me off; when he activated me the second time we talked about Earth.

But the trouble was, neither of us knew much about it, so we built one to suit our own fancies.

It was a harmless pastime, and after we had slept again

it was time to make our move, and the boredom was over. Paul told me where the skimmer was, and we timed it so that I would reach the place in the middle of the night when everyone should be asleep.

As I got ready to go, Paul began digging in the cupboard he had built for our supplies.

"What are you doing?" I asked.

He straightened up, grinning. "As long as things are going to work out so well, I'll eat the rest of the food."

I didn't object. I left the cave thinking of a word he'd tried to teach me. The word was "optimist." I hadn't been able to get much of a grasp on what it meant. But now I was beginning to.

We had very good luck at the start. I got the skimmer without any trouble at all and left the money Paul gave me under a rock when I took it. We had discussed leaving some kind of a note also, but we decided that would have been a little too honest.

I brought the skimmer back to the cave, and we started for Ganapolis right away. This would be the touchy part, avoiding detection during the trip. The hunting parties would be watching for skimmers.

We didn't see any hunting parties and decided we'd been right — that three days of unsuccessful search had discouraged most of them.

I was getting pretty hungry when Ganapolis came in sight, but I didn't say anything about it to Paul because I saw no point in worrying him. We would get a charge as soon as we could; of course, if we were unable to find one — well, it was a useless thing to worry about.

Ganapolis is the biggest city on Ganymede. It looks like all other cities, I suppose. The business section has a bubble over it, with people entering through a dozen air locks.

Much of the city is exposed, however, with the residences underground, and it looks a lot like the residential section at the colony, only a lot bigger.

We parked the skimmer beside a lot of others, and I asked Paul, "What will we do now?"

"We'll go into the domed section, and I'll try to buy you a charge."

"The chances are pretty slim, don't you think?"

"They'll probably be suspicious, but —"

"They'll probably grab a gun and blow my head off. They've all heard the news."

"But we've got to take a chance. You need a charge!"

"You can say that again. I'm getting awfully sleepy. But I've got a better idea. I saw an old, battered Class 3 space freighter when we passed the port."

"So?"

"A lot of those old space rats don't pay much attention to local news."

"We'll go out there and ask the captain for a charge?"

"Not quite like that," I said. "They're loading the ship, and that gave me the idea. He might get suspicious if you just walk up and ask."

"What's your idea?"

"Let's get started. I'll tell you on the way."

I was fighting sleep. It was getting close to the end for me, and I had to concentrate on what I told Paul to make sure I didn't ramble. When a robot's charge is almost gone, it gets light-headed sometimes and says crazy things.

But I got the idea over to Paul, and a little while later we walked up to the ship I had in mind, a battered old hulk named the *Terrabella*.

This was it. Now I could only stand and wait.

7. Stowaway

"**W**ANT TO RENT ANOTHER ROBOT?"
I watched as Paul sauntered up to the man standing by the *Terrabella*'s pilot port and asked the question eagerly. The man squinted his small, suspicious eyes at Paul and answered, "Huh?"

"I asked if you want to rent another robot. I see you're loading. You *are* the captain, aren't you?"

"I am! Owner, captain, pilot, general handyman of the *Terrabella*, the best freighter in the planetary trade. She'll go anywhere and carry anything!"

He was a belligerent little man — I think that's the word — with a fringe of white hair around a bald head. His skin was weather-beaten into a mass of deep wrinkles, and his short, wide body looked strong enough to lift one end of the ship.

Paul stared at the ship with bright eyes. He was trying to look younger than he really was — a boy with a robot, perhaps his father's robot — who was trying to earn a little money around the spaceport by renting the robot out.

This was what we were trying to make the captain think, but I couldn't tell whether we were succeeding or not. Paul and I were certainly a logical pair to find around a busy spaceport.

"Well," Paul demanded, "do you want to rent him?"

"Name's Becker," the man said. "Captain Becker." He rubbed his hand along his space helmet, revealing a habit of rubbing his jaw when he was pondering a problem. He looked back toward the freight ports where the loading was going on — crates and boxes for the interplanetary trade.

"Got me three good loading robots now."

"You're running shorthanded," Paul said casually. "A ship of this size would normally use five."

Captain Becker looked at Paul approvingly. His mouth twisted into a crooked grin. "H'm-m-m-m — you're a pretty smart young'un."

Paul's knowledge wasn't surprising. He loved spaceships. He'd built models, and had spent quite a lot of time there at the Ganapolis port.

He shrugged. "It's up to you," he said indifferently. "But make up your mind. If you don't want my robot, I'll go try another ship."

"Spunky too, I see. What would be your idea of a fair rental?"

Paul shrugged again. He gestured toward me. "Needs a charge," he said. "Give me one, and I'll —"

"Oh, needs a charge, huh? That makes it a little different."

I was almost through, fighting to hold consciousness on the last dregs in my batteries. I wondered if I'd be there to hear the finish of it.

"A charge would have to come out of the rent," Captain Becker said.

"I'd expect it to," Paul said with spirit.

Then there was a gap. I lost consciousness. My metal body stiffened into rigidity of course, and I didn't know anything more until I heard Paul say, "All right, he's ready to go to work now," and saw him close the door of my torso box. I knew we'd made it. I had a charge.

I watched as Captain Becker took my dead batteries into the ship to put them into the charger, and while he was gone Paul turned to me and whispered, "It worked, Rex. And I found out some other things. This ship is about ready to head in for Mars. After that — Earth. Let's try to stow away on her!"

Even if I hadn't agreed, it would not have mattered. The tone of Paul's suggestion made it an order. He hadn't put it as a question, nor had he left any room for discussion. The tone of voice is the main factor in a robot's command response.

"All right," I said.

We had no time to make plans, because Captain Becker came right back out.

"We're wasting time here," he said. "I'm paying good money for that robot, and I want some work out of him."

"What do you want him to do?" Paul asked.

"Load! What else? Tell him to help carry those boxes and crates into the hold."

Paul pointed to the stack of cargo and snapped, "Go to work, Rex."

I instantly obeyed the command, walking to the rear of the ship where the three loading robots were carrying boxes up the ramp.

They were primitive types — the kind you would naturally find on an old tub like the *Terrabella,* just as Captain Becker was the kind of captain who would be working such a ship.

There were many such tramp cargo carriers on the outerplanetary freight runs — most of them Class 3's — and usually all battered to pieces, because the Class 3 was the most durable ship ever made. They operated off force fields instead of rocket tubes, and there was very little about them that could go out of order.

I learned all that from Paul, who got it from reading books. It had been said of the Class 3's that they didn't have to be retired until nothing but a couple of bolts and a strip of hull floated into port.

They were called one-man ships, because a captain who knew his business needed only a crew of robots to roam the spaceways wherever he chose.

But they were terribly slow. That was their drawback. Their force fields lifted them beyond the drag of their port-of-call planet, and they plodded along the freight lanes like old men going home from a hard day's work.

That was what it said in one of Paul's books, and of course I remember it.

The *Terrabella* was about eighty feet in diameter and ninety feet in height, and since it landed through atmosphere it had stubby guide fins and a tapered nose.

I got in line with the other robots and picked up one of the crates and walked up the ramp into the hold. The crates were being stacked neatly from the back bulkhead forward, and while I worked I thought about how Paul and I could stow away on the ship.

He was still talking to Captain Becker as I came down the ramp, and when I picked up my second crate they went in through the pilot port together and I decided Paul must have asked to see the ship.

He could have been very sincere about asking that, because he loved spaceships and everything about them.

I kept on working, unable to plan anything for Paul until I found out how things were breaking for him. Maybe he had a plan of his own.

There was about three hours' work left before the hold would be sealed, and I hoped he would be able to get to me before it was finished.

I kept on working until finally the pilot port opened and Paul and Captain Becker came out. They stood by the hull talking a while, and then Captain Becker went away.

Paul immediately came back to the cargo pile.

"What happened?" I asked.

"I told him I was hungry, and he gave me something to eat. He's a nice guy when you get to know him."

"How about stowing away? Have you got a plan?"

I picked up a crate, and we started walking toward the ramp. Paul frowned and scratched his helmet over his chin the way I'd seen Captain Becker do. Evidently the captain impressed Paul.

"Things don't look good," Paul said. "He keeps the pilot lock closed to conserve air. I can't go in without his being there. How about the cargo hold?"

"There's no place to hide in there except maybe in a crate, and that would be very dangerous."

Paul knew what I meant. There was enough air in his suit to last a little while, and he could generate a reasonable amount of heat in it. But if he got trapped in the cargo hold of the *Terrabella* and couldn't get out after take-off, he would be frozen stiff in subzero space temperatures long before his air gave out.

"The hold hatch won't be locked, will it?"

"It isn't locked now," I said, "but you never can tell what Becker's routine is. A couple of hours would freeze you to death if he locked it before take-off."

Paul knew that was absolute truth too. Becker would have to have access to the cargo hold, but he might lock the hatch and not go in there for days.

Paul walked back and forth with me on two trips. He remained silent, deep in thought. Then his eyes brightened, and I could see that the spirit and the excitement of the adventure were gripping him.

"Can you get me into one of those crates?"

I wanted to lie and say that I couldn't, but that was not possible. A robot cannot consciously lie. Truth, through automatic obedience, is built into us.

"I wouldn't advise it," I said.

"I asked you, Rex, can you get me into one of those crates?"

"I think so."

"How?"

"I can go around behind the pile and open one and empty it. You could climb in, and I could seal it again and carry it in. But I wouldn't advise doing that."

"We'll take a chance," Paul said.

"What if you can't get out of the hold?"

"You're going to be aboard, aren't you? You can let me out."

"Do you think we're just going to walk in there and take Captain Becker's ship over?"

"Rex! If we're going to get anywhere, we've got to take some chances."

"But —"

"Get the box ready."

He turned and walked away. I, of course, had to accept that as an order.

On the next trip I went around behind the pile and picked one of the larger boxes. Clawing the top off wasn't any trouble, but I had to carry the contents over and drop them behind someone else's pile of cargo. The contents were tightly pressed packages of dried herbs, and while I was moving them it occurred to me that it wasn't quite honest, throwing a man's cargo around like that.

But I had an order, so I didn't think too much about it. This was different from our talk about the skimmer back in the cave. Paul hadn't put the command tone into any of his words then.

After I had emptied the box, I made another trip into the hold with the other robots, and then Paul came back and ducked behind the cargo pile.

I followed him, and when he had jumped into the box I nailed the lid back on. After that, it was simple. I picked up the box and carried it into the hold.

I put it against the forward bulkhead — not with the rest that were being put on top of each other from back to front.

And I hoped it would be allowed to stay there.

But it wasn't.

Five minutes later Captain Becker came back from wherever he had gone and climbed the ramp and looked into the hold. I followed him in with a box of cargo, and when I'd put it where it belonged he pointed to the box Paul was in.

"What's that doing there?"

"I brought it in," I said.

"Put it where it should be! Why's it standing out there?"

I wanted to tell him I put it out there because Paul was in it, and if it got stuck in with the others he would freeze to death, but of course I couldn't. All I could do was put it where he told me and go back after another crate.

Captain Becker stood beside the ramp now, squinting at us as we loaded the cargo. "Let's step it up here," he said. "Let's get this cargo in. I want to get off this satellite. Let's step it up."

The robots kept on going at their regular pace as Captain Becker had fully expected them to. Their speed was preset. He knew that and was only talking to relieve his own impatience.

When there were only a few boxes left, he gave an order to one of the robots to finish the loading and then to board the ship and wait. "I'll seal the port after I get back with the manifests."

My problem was solved. While Captain Becker was away getting his manifests, I would climb into the cargo hold and hide behind the crates. He would come back and look in and see the robots inside, and would then go in through the pilot port and lock the freight port from up there.

Maybe he would leave the cargo hatch open, and we would be able to get forward and try to find a place to stow away. But even if he locked it before take-off, everything would still be all right.

Before I'd let Paul freeze to death I'd break the hatch open and take him forward.

So everything was all right.

Or at least I thought it was.

But it wasn't.

Captain Becker turned back after taking three steps and called out, "You — Rex — come with me."

I walked to where he was.

"I want you to go with me," he said. "You'll find a box on a chair in the pilot's cabin. I left the port unlocked. Get it and close the port. It's a little present for the dispatcher. You carry it for me."

I did as he ordered, thinking that if only we'd done nothing at all, Paul could have gone in the pilot's port and stowed away with no trouble at all, now that the port was unlocked. But he couldn't do that. He was nailed in a box in the cargo hold.

And if I couldn't figure out a way to get on the ship, he would freeze to death.

8. Bound for Mars

I WENT TO THE DISPATCHER'S OFFICE with Captain Becker, and after I put the package on the desk I stepped back toward the wall and waited while the captain got his manifests and talked to the port dispatcher.

No one paid any attention to me. Not that I was afraid they would. It would have been hard for anyone to associate a mad robot and a kidnaped boy with an old space captain and a robot that carried packages for him.

I was worried about something else, and now I knew what worry really was. Strange, unhappy thoughts and conflicts were pitching around in my control box. There would be no danger of Paul's freezing to death. No danger at all. I would try to get onto the *Terrabella* with him, but if I couldn't I would simply tell Captain Becker that Paul was stowed away in his cargo hold, and he would get Paul out of there.

Simple.

Except that I knew I couldn't do it.

That was what scared me. I suppose to you, a human, that seems silly, and I doubt if I can make you understand by telling you a robot just isn't patterned to disobey a command. Not a normal, correctly functioning robot.

There is a very good reason for this. Robots are built to take orders from humans, which is as it should be. And it wouldn't make any sense to give robots the power to pass on human orders. If they were allowed to do that, they wouldn't be trustworthy.

I had the mental capacity for only one course. Paul had ordered me to put him aboard the *Terrabella* and then to get aboard myself. Therefore I had to try to carry out the last part of the order.

I quit thinking about Paul freezing to death in the hold of that ship and concentrated on getting aboard myself. I concentrated hard, even though the project seemed impossible.

First, I knew Captain Becker wouldn't be fool enough to let me take off with him just because I asked him to. That would be stealing a robot, and it would put him in real trouble when he returned to Ganapolis on his next trip. He wouldn't dare do that, no matter how hard a bargainer he was.

When we got back to the ship, he would decide that Paul had grown tired of waiting and had gone home, and he would send me home too. He had paid a very small rental for me and had gotten a lot of work done, so he would be satisfied.

Hopeless — but I kept thinking about it. I thought hard

as we walked back to the ship, and two things about Captain Becker kept repeating themselves.

A hard bargainer. A small rental.

These two things were true. He was a hard bargainer, because he had gotten me for a very small rental.

And that gave me an idea. I didn't know whether it would work, but I could try it.

"The two robots that you are short," I said, "are they in the repair shop?"

"Back in Marsport," he grumbled. "They weren't ready when I left, and I didn't want to miss this run, so I took a chance."

"That was risky. A one-man ship can go to pieces if the crew is short."

"The *Terrabella* went to pieces years ago," he growled. "She just doesn't know it yet."

"That fin up there needs a repair job," I said, pointing to it. "The alloy skin is going to tear off."

His eyes darted in my direction. "Are you patterned for repair work?"

"Skilled repairs. I can fix watches and even radios."

"And I had you carrying cargo," he said with disgust. "Why didn't that kid tell me you were skilled?"

"You didn't ask him."

He scowled at me, but we had reached the ship and he squinted at it as he checked things over. The robots were not in sight. Evidently they had finished loading and were in the cargo hold as he had ordered.

He strode to the hold and went up the ramp and peered in. "Hey! Boy! You in there?"

He could see the whole interior from the port, so he

didn't go in. He yelled once more for Paul, and then came down and pulled the ramp clear.

"That kid didn't wait," he growled. "You'd better go find him and get him on home, or his old man will larrup him."

"But he rented me to you," I said.

This was it. I would get on the *Terrabella* now or I wouldn't. It all depended on how Captain Becker reacted.

He gave me a quick, angular look and snorted. "The work's done. I'm clearing gravity. I've got no further use for you."

"What about that fin? And your short crew. You rented me, didn't you? And I haven't been released."

"Are you trying to talk me into stealing you?"

"How is it stealing? You made a deal. No time limit was set, was there?"

He looked at me steadily, and I knew his mind was working fast. "You've got a restless streak in you, Rex. You want to travel, don't you?"

"I'm not a runaway, if that's what you mean. But there *was* a rental deal."

"Sure. I take you with me, and the deal is that I get smacked with a heavy fine and maybe jail when I come back here."

"Why? Haven't you got a right to take rented property with you as long as you bring it back?"

"The kid would say it was only for the afternoon."

"He might be mad, but he wouldn't say that. He's not a liar."

"What about his father?"

"He isn't here. He went to Earth on business."

"H'm-m-m. No wonder the kid's around renting you out." He thought for a while, and I could see that he was weakening. "When I get back, he'll probably ask for more rent."

"Maybe I'd be worth it."

"You say you can do skilled repairs?" He asked the question again, as though he needed a last little bit of reassurance before taking a chance.

"Yes."

"All right. Get aboard — through the pilot port — and let's climb out of here."

If I'd been a human and needed air, I would have taken a deep breath of it right there. As it was, my relays buzzed a little from the excitement and the satisfaction as I climbed into the pilot's cabin and watched Captain Becker secure the ship.

It didn't take long. The ports clanked to in response to their signals, and green lights went on all across the board and we began to lift. We lifted slowly at first, then faster and faster, and when we were clear of gravity, I looked down and saw that I had two of the steel fingers on my right hand crossed the way Paul did so often.

I uncrossed them and said, "Is it all right if I look the ship over?"

"Go ahead," Captain Becker grunted. "I'd just as soon have your weight aft for a while."

I left the pilot's cabin in a hurry, my control box singing with satisfaction. It could not have worked out better. I knew Captain Becker would stay at the controls until he got the course laid out and had checked the automatics.

76

That would give me time to get Paul out of the cargo hold and into a safe place forward.

We'd certainly had more luck than we were entitled to.

And it hadn't run out yet — the luck, I mean. The *Terrabella* was laid out to handle a bigger human crew than Captain Becker ever used. Or maybe the empty cabins — six of them along the companionway — were for passengers in case he could find any foolish enough to ride such a junk of a ship.

Anyhow, four of them were padlocked and dusty enough to show that Captain Becker hadn't entered them in months. I picked one of them and broke the padlock carefully, so that I could push the curved bar back into its hole and make it look as though it hadn't been tampered with.

Then I went and got Paul.

He was glad to see me, but he wasn't at all worried. "It took you quite a while," he said casually, and I had to envy humans because they were so intelligent. Paul had said everything would work out, and it did. That was what came of having a human brain, I told myself. And I felt ashamed for not having had more confidence in him. The first thing a robot should realize is that a human can always be trusted. I resolved not to let that get lost in my memory bank again.

"I'm hungry," Paul said when I had him safely in the unused cabin. "Can you find me something to eat?"

He had taken his suit off, but he was shaking a little bit — nowhere near frozen or anything like that, but the subzero temperatures penetrate the hull of the freight hold on a cargo spacer pretty fast.

"You get warm," I said. "I'll go to the galley and bring something back."

The galley was between the cabins and the part of the ship where Captain Becker was. I went there and gathered up enough food to last Paul a couple of days. I didn't have to carry water because there was a faucet in Paul's cabin, and water came in direct from the distilling unit.

"You won't be able to take a bath," I told Paul. "Captain Becker won't miss the drinking water, but if you used more he'd probably start looking for a leak."

Paul was cramming bread into his mouth. It was so full I could hardly understand him when he asked, "Did you have a hard time getting aboard?"

"No. I'm a working robot on the Mars run. He's short-handed and needs me."

"It's going to be tough, cramped in here all that time."

The run from Jupiter to Mars is the longest on the space-ways, especially in an old tub like the *Terrabella*. It takes many days. Paul was right, and there was nothing I could do about it. He could have walked out and claimed stow-away's work privileges, and Captain Becker would prob-ably have given them to him. But we would certainly have landed in the hands of the Martian police when we reached Mars and have been separated very quickly.

Captain Becker had too much sense to lay himself open to a kidnaping charge.

At least I thought he did.

"There are lots of books and magazines aboard," I told Paul. "And I'll come here whenever I can."

"Where's Captain Becker now? Laying his course, I suppose?"

"Yes. It will take him at least another hour."

Paul's first hunger gone, he began picking thoughtfully at his food. "Well," he said, "we got on this ship. I wonder what's next. But this is a real break. We're going to get to Earth after all."

"And when we get there —"

"It may be a little rough. Earth is a big planet. It's got more ports than any other. It depends on where we put down. If we get a bad break that way, we could be as badly off as we were on Ganymede."

"Is that possible?"

"Sure. Suppose Captain Becker takes this crate to one of the Arctic or Antarctic ports? Maybe he plans to pick up a cargo of pelts from one of the big polar fur farms. We'd be really stuck."

"We might have to jump ship at Mars."

"We'll have to wait and find out."

"Are they as hard on robots on Earth as they are on Ganymede?"

"What do you mean?"

"Perhaps they won't shoot me down. I've heard Earth is an enlightened planet."

"It is, but not so far as mad robots are concerned."

That made me sad. What good was enlightenment if it wasn't going to help us?

"Maybe they won't get the word at all the Earth ports — about us, about me kidnaping you?"

"They will in all the big ones. Interplanetary Security takes care of things like that, and they're very efficient."

I had a thought about that too. If they were so efficient, how come a boy and a robot could stow away on a space freighter under conditions that even an automatic guard robot would have been suspicious of? I didn't think about that very long, because when one human calls another human efficient, this is the absolute truth, because humans always know what they are talking about, and my logic was faulty.

Paul lay back on his bunk and took a deep, satisfied breath. "Everything's going to be all right," he said.

"But you just told me —"

"I mean in the long-range planning department. Our long-range planning was perfect."

"Was it?"

"Of course. We're on a ship bound for Earth, aren't we?"

I certainly couldn't get around that. Still, it seemed to me that a lot of other factors had been involved. I couldn't remember our discussing long-range plans to a point of getting to Earth. We had mentioned a spaceship, however, and here it was. I decided long-range planning was a pretty good thing.

"All perfect," Paul said. "When we get home, Dad will have to agree that I'm grown up now and can take care of myself. Planning and executing this trip proves that. He'll have to respect me. And he'll have to let me keep you."

"Do you still have the money you're going to send back to Mr. Hennings? He'll insist on that."

Paul patted his pocket. "I have it," he said.

"I'd better go back. I don't want Captain Becker to get suspicious. I'll come again as soon as I can."

I left the cabin and fixed the padlock so it didn't look tampered with. I even got some dust — there was plenty of that around — and sprinkled it on the padlock.

It was important to keep in good with Captain Becker, so I stopped in the galley and made a cup of coffee and took it up to him.

He looked up from his plotting board and squinted at me when I got there and then he snorted.

"Well, aren't you a one! Who told you to make that coffee?"

"Nobody. It comes from the conditioning of living with a family. I have impression retention units in my —"

"Spare the details," he grunted as he waved a hand in protest. "The point is, can you make good coffee?"

He tasted the coffee and snorted again. But a different kind of snort this time, one of appreciation. "Are you a cook too?"

"I have transferred the contents of two cookbooks into my memory bank and —"

"Spare me, spare me! From now on, you're the cook. Go bring me another cup of coffee."

I went to get it, and I was very glad things had worked out this way. As cook, I could see to it Paul got all the food he needed during the run.

I poured the coffee and had to admit that you couldn't beat long-range planning.

81

9. The Long Jump

Out in the black reaches of space, time means little.

THAT WAS A LINE FROM ONE of Paul's books, a line I liked because it gave me a kind of a feeling I couldn't understand. Still, I knew it was a feeling.

I'd never thought I would sometime be experiencing what the line meant. But on the run from Ganymede to Mars on Captain Becker's *Terrabella,* I got the idea.

It was as though you didn't need time any more. What good was it? The void around you was always dark. The Sun neither came up nor went down. The same things happened during any given hour that had happened the hour before and would happen during the next hour.

One thing I noticed: as the days went by I developed a very big respect for the ship I rode in, even if it was the lumbering old *Terrabella* — a respect, and maybe even an affection, though I don't know. I don't think I know what affection is.

But I knew how I felt about the *Terrabella*. In port, she was just an old tub of a spacer that nobody would look at twice. But out in the void, she was everything. There she came into her own.

Somehow, for me, she took on the same personality as her owner, Captain Becker, grunting and snorting and grumbling along, not paying any attention to anything, just interested in getting to where she was going — into another spaceport — so she could sit down and rest for a while before they made her get out and bumble along the spaceways again.

I thought I felt grateful to the old *Terrabella*, but I probably didn't. Certainly not the way humans feel gratitude. What I felt was probably some by-product of my self-preservation quotient. The *Terrabella* was preserving me from destruction. I suppose I appreciated it as much as a soulless mechanism can appreciate anything.

But I do know this — when Captain Becker sent me out to repair the damaged landing fin, I did the job very carefully, because it was a very personal job. I wanted the fin to be exactly right — as right as anything I had ever done.

Of course a human can't go out on the hull of a ship during free fall, but it's nothing for a robot. No, I guess I shouldn't say that. Humans do go out, under vital emergency conditions, and make voidside repairs on a ship.

But they have to have the best of equipment — specially constructed space suits and all the rest of it.

But it's very dangerous and is not done unless survival is involved.

But to me it was nothing at all. I merely screwed on a pair of magnetic shoes and went out the cargo lock while the other robots stood by to see that none of the cargo came loose and floated out the lock into the void.

I remember that I took a long time repairing the fin, longer than I really needed, because I enjoyed being out there by myself. I got a feeling of *splendid isolation*. I think that's what it was. I always liked words, and those two came from one of Paul's books. *Splendid isolation*. I had always thought that words were things people felt as well as said, otherwise there wouldn't be any point to them. And I was always trying to feel what I thought the words meant.

And out there, voidside, there was just the *Terrabella* and me, and nothing else had ever been made or ever would be. I wanted to talk to her and ask her how she felt, hauling freight up and down the spaceways for Captain Becker.

I did ask her, as a matter of fact, but she only grunted and went wallowing on toward Mars.

I got an impression about the *Terrabella*. I think she was a little cruel. I don't think she cared much about anything. I think she would just as soon have dumped Captain Becker out a port and left him pawing around in space as not. I hoped she didn't feel that way about me.

All of which must sound pretty silly to you, a human,

But you must remember that a robot can be a pretty silly mechanism at times.

I did a lot of work on the *Terrabella*, but it was all right — I liked it. I fixed Captain Becker's chronometers and repaired the electronic heating system and reinforced some of the pressure tanks.

And I cleaned the place. I cleaned and cleaned and cleaned until Captain Becker began to complain about my using too much water. So I used less water, making one pail do until it was nothing but mud.

Also, I did the cooking, which satisfied Captain Becker very much. And it satisfied me, because that way I could see that Paul got everything he needed to eat.

Another thing: I worked on the other robots too. I cleaned them and polished them until they looked the way I liked to look myself, their metal shining and their duller box surfaces glowing clean.

Captain Becker complained about that.

"What are you doing, Rex? It's getting so I can't tell you from the others. I asked X-7 to bring me a cup of coffee the other day and he kept saying, 'Reword the order. Reword the order,' and I thought your relays had gone bad."

That is what a robot says when an order doesn't register correctly or when it is beyond the robot's capacity to obey.

The other robots did look like me. We were exact duplicates outside. It was the inside that was different. They were patterned with cheap, elemental circuits that responded to only the most basic commands.

"You could have read his serial number," I said.

"Why should I go around reading serial numbers on my own ship? You just let me know when it's you. Blow a whistle or something."

I didn't have a whistle and I didn't think there was one on the ship, but I said, "Yes, sir," anyhow because it wouldn't be difficult to let Captain Becker know he was talking to me. I fixed it by tying a string around one of the arms of each of the other robots. A very simple solution to the problem that even a robot could figure out.

And one that even a snorting old space tramp could use to his advantage. But I didn't like that thought when it came. A robot shouldn't have such thoughts about humans.

Besides, Captain Becker had a nice side to him. He wasn't as bad as he appeared on the outside. When things were quiet and there was nothing to be done, we sat and talked a lot, and I'm sure he liked my company.

I found out that he knew a lot more than he appeared to, especially about music. This was his big interest, and was why he didn't even have a functioning radio aboard until I fixed an old one I found in the galley. He had his music tapes and spent all his spare time with them.

One day when we were talking he asked me if I liked music, and then played one of his tapes for me. It had a strange sound.

"Do robots know what rhythm is?" he asked me.

"Rhythm is an even beat."

"That's rhythm that you're listening to."

"It isn't even."

"It doesn't have to be. That's authentic Venusian. It

86

was taped at a ritual of a Kiba tribe in the equatorial jungle. The Kibas can do weird things with rhythm. Their tapes are prohibited on Mars because they do strange things to Martians — drive them crazy. Martians go for them like Terrans go for drugs."

"Would that one drive a Martian crazy?"

"If he listened to it long enough. The Venusians can drug themselves by blending rhythms with bright colors."

"I can't see colors."

"Your refractor bulb is for black and white?"

"Yes."

He scratched his chin. "Wait a minute. I think maybe I've got something for you. There's an old box of spare parts in my cabin — "

He went away, and when he came back he had a refractor bulb in his hand. "Don't know where I picked this thing up. It's been around for a long time. Maybe it won't work."

Then I had one of the most exciting moments of my life — when he took my old tube out and put the other one in.

I haven't got the words to describe how I felt. It was like seeing a new world even there in his dingy cabin.

"Everything's different!" I cried.

He squinted at me and grinned, and I could see that he was pleased. "I guess it would be. That's color you're seeing. My shirt's blue. The paint on that chair is red. Not too bright. You'll see lots brighter colors than that."

"It's — wonderful!"

"Why don't you take a look outside?"

I went into the pilot's cabin in the nose of the *Terrabella* to get a better view, and for a while I couldn't say anything. I just stared.

The stars had changed. All those white specks were different. They were red and blue, and they all seemed to have come to life. There were other colors too — colors I didn't know the names of.

"Even the black of the void is different," I said. "It's a color too."

He had followed me in, enjoying my amazement. "It's still black," he said. "Black's the absence of color. But I suppose it does look more alive to you."

"Can — may I keep it?"

"The bulb? Sure. I have no use for it."

I laughed, and it was the first time since I'd been made that my laugh wasn't in response to the laughter of a human. It came from me, from the wonder of seeing color.

"I've got a lot of looking to do," I said.

"Then you'd better get at it."

I stood there and kept looking out at the beautiful sky. In a little while I heard a new tape going, and I knew Captain Becker had gone back to his music.

I had to tell Paul. That was the thought I had. I left the pilot's cabin and went back to where he was stowed away.

It had been pretty hard on Paul. He was a boy, and boys get restless with nothing to do but read books and magazines.

I tried to be with him as much as possible, but I had

to be very careful. He understood this, but when it was time to leave him he would always ask me to stay a little longer.

I opened the fake padlock on his door and went in and found him reading a book. He threw it down and looked at me sullenly.

"I'm getting tired of trade magazines on space and association bulletins. Hasn't Captain Becker got books on anything but music and space travel?"

"I'll see if I can find some," I said. "In the meantime I ought to wash your shirt. The red's getting a little dingy."

He missed it at first. Then he jerked his eyes back to me and said, "What do you mean — red?"

"That blue bedspread could do with a washing too," I said.

"What's wrong with you? Have you gone space-happy? You don't know colors."

"I do now. Captain Becker had a color refractor bulb aboard, and he gave it to me."

"I told you I'd get you one," he said, and I think he was a little angry.

"I'd rather use yours, Paul," I said, "but is it all right if I keep this one until we get to where you can buy me the one you had in mind?"

"Oh, I suppose so. But I'm beginning to wonder if we'll ever get to a place like that. This tub must be standing still in space."

"Oh, it's moving," I assured him. "But it's a very slow ship."

"You're telling me!"

"It's pretty hard on you, I know."

"Hard! I'm bored stiff!"

Then, very suddenly, nobody was bored any more.

Everything changed, because the cabin door opened at that moment and Captain Becker stepped into the cabin and stood there staring at Paul.

10. Mars Landing

"WHAT'S THIS? What's been going on here?"

Captain Becker threw those questions at us as he stood there with his little eyes all squinty and his face full of rage. You could see that he was mad and scared — a Captain Becker we hadn't seen before.

"I'm a stowaway on your ship," Paul said.

"Any fool can see that! What I want to know is, did you think I was such an idiot I wouldn't find you?"

"You almost didn't," Paul said defiantly.

I knew he didn't feel defiant. He was scared too, and was trying to act brave.

Captain Becker turned on me. "You think you're a real smart robot, don't you? You set all this up. The kid hasn't got the brains."

This made Paul really mad. "Are you saying I'm not as smart as a robot?"

"I'm saying you're both a pair of idiots to think you could get away with this. I've been too long on the space-ways to get exiled on some stinking asteroid for kidnaping."

"Kidnaping?" From the way Paul spoke the word, I knew he was stalling for time — trying to think of something. I knew that the idea of Captain Becker's being charged with kidnaping hadn't occurred to him.

It hadn't occurred to me either. Paul was a stowaway, and that was that. It had happened before on the space-ways — reckless kids hunting for adventure.

"That's foolish," I said. "They won't — "

"Oh, won't they? They can say I got control of you on Ganymede and sent you to kidnap the boy — maybe for the slave trade out in the Asteroid Belt. Or even for ransom, he being a governor's son!"

This was a new angle. Captain Becker must have known about us all the time.

"Where did you hear the story about Rex kidnaping me?" Paul asked in amazement.

"Never mind where I heard it. I'm asking the questions here!"

"You had to find out about it before we left Ganymede. You've had no communication since you took off."

If that was true, I thought, Captain Becker had been pretty stupid not to be suspicious of us when we approached him. Under those conditions they might charge him with being in on the supposed kidnaping. But I was sure he wouldn't have taken me aboard if he had known.

Suddenly I remembered. The radio I'd fixed! While I'd been in there telling Paul about my new color bulb, he

92

must have turned that radio on and heard the news about us on some Interplanetary Security broadcast.

"It's true, isn't it?" Captain Becker asked. "You are Paul Simpson, aren't you? And Rex is the robot they were talking about?"

I didn't see how Paul could cover it up any longer, and neither did he, because he said, "Yes, that part is true, but the rest of it — about the kidnaping — is all wrong. Rex didn't kidnap me. I sneaked off the *Star Queen* by myself. If anything, I stole him from the man my father sold him to on Ganymede."

Captain Becker's little eyes popped wide open. His bald head was bright red, and he was almost jumping up and down in anger.

"That's just as bad," he howled. "They can say I talked you into stealing him for me and then gave you a lift off Ganymede. Either way, it's the Asteroids!"

Paul stared in amazement at Captain Becker's new explosion of anger.

I waited for one of them to say something, and when they didn't I decided it would be all right for me to make a suggestion.

"As long as neither story is true, perhaps you'd be smarter to break the radio again and say you hadn't heard anything about a kidnaping. We haven't been traced to your ship, or there would be an Interplanetary Control Squad alongside by now."

"Are you trying to get me in even deeper?" Captain Becker yelled.

Paul picked the idea up quickly. "That doesn't get you

in deeper. It gets you out! All Rex and I were trying to do in the first place was to get to the Earth. That's where you're going, so what's the problem? Take us to an Earth spaceport, and we'll slip away and you won't be involved."

"What's your port of call on Earth?" I asked.

"Kansas City," he answered absently, his mind appearing to have gone into low gear.

But then it moved back into high gear again. "Look here! I said *I* was asking the questions. And that idea stinks. When they find you on Earth, you think Interplanetary isn't going to want to know how you got there? And you think they aren't going to find out? My only chance — and it's a slim one — is to drop you at my first port of call, Marsport. I'll turn you over to the Martian police and tell them the truth — that I got the story on my radio after I cleared Ganymede. It's the truth, and maybe they'll believe it."

"Why shouldn't they believe all the truth when we tell them that there never was a kidnaping?"

I asked him that, although it wouldn't have helped me any. Not much anyhow. They would ship me back to Ganymede to Mr. Hennings and send Paul to his father.

No, it didn't help much. Not the way I felt then. I could see color. I'd had a big taste of freedom. And going back to Ganymede where I would never see Paul again would be about as bad as being shot for a mad robot.

"There doesn't have to be any trouble at all," Paul said. "Not if you'll listen to reason. In fact, you can end up getting a reward."

"Who will give me a reward for breaking every interplanetary law on the books?"

94

"My father. I'll contact him as soon as we get to Earth, and he'll be so glad to see me he'll reward you for bringing me to him."

Captain Becker scowled. "If I was your dad, I'd warm your pants till you couldn't sit down."

"Maybe he'll do that too," Paul said. "But he'll still be glad."

For the first time Captain Becker seemed undecided what to do, and Paul pushed his advantage. "Tell you what — I'll pay our passage, Rex's and mine."

"Sure," Captain Becker snorted, "with Ganymedian pennies?"

"I've got plenty of money. Five thousand Earth dollars."

"Where'd you get that kind of money? Did you rob a bank as well as steal a robot?"

"It's honest money!" Paul said angrily. "My father gave it to me."

He pulled a wad of currency out of his jacket pocket, and I hadn't known before that Captain Becker's eyes could open so wide. They almost popped out of his bald head.

"Great jets, what's the younger generation coming to?" he snorted. "Roaming around the System carrying that kind of money!"

It was easy to see that he liked money very much.

"It's twice what I need to buy first-class tickets for both of us."

Captain Becker leaned back on the bulkhead and scratched his chin. The money was a great temptation to him. Then he straightened up decisively.

"Plenty of time to think about that. We're still fifteen

days out of Marsport. And right now you're going to be treated like any other stowaway. You got certain rights and privileges, and one of them is to work and keep on working some more. Get yourself a bucket and a brush, and start scrubbing the companionway."

I automatically turned toward the bucket, but Captain Becker held up his hand. "Not you, Rex. This youngster needs a lesson. He'll do his work himself. He's not the son of a rich man with a robot to wipe his nose for him. Not on this ship he's not. You get into the galley and see about mess. One thing you two are going to find out is that I'm captain of this ship."

So that was how it was left — fifteen days out of Marsport — with Paul and me a little nervous about what Captain Becker would do when we got there, but with pretty much of a feeling that he would give in and take us to Earth.

"He won't be able to pass the money up," Paul said when I went back into the companionway to see how the scrubbing was coming along. "He's a born slave driver. Every muscle in my body aches," he added.

"It looks as though your long-range planning worked out pretty well," I said.

He gave me a disgusted look. "I didn't plan this."

"Nothing is ever absolutely perfect."

I felt bad, seeing Paul work that way, but there was nothing I could do about it except see to it that he got good nourishing meals. I encouraged him as best I could.

"It won't be forever. Marsport is coming closer and closer."

96

"Sure, but I didn't plan on scrubbing my way there."

Captain Becker didn't have much to say for a while. He listened to his music and read his books, and when I tried to strike up conversations, he stopped me with a grunt and a couple of snorts, so I let him alone.

He paid no attention to Paul, acting as though he wasn't even on the ship, except when he checked his work and laid out more for him.

One day when he had turned off a tape of weird Martian hill music, he squinted at me suddenly and said, "Regular fare isn't enough."

"Paul didn't mean unscheduled freighter fare," I said. "He meant first-class luxury-liner ticket prices."

"It still isn't enough. I'm taking an awful risk."

"Shall I call him in?"

"I guess you'd better."

I went and got Paul, telling him on the way forward what Captain Becker had said. "The old bandit," Paul muttered. "I'll bet he would kidnap slaves for the Asteroid Belt at that."

"I don't think he has that idea about us."

Paul squinted at me and scowled a little like Captain Becker.

"They buy robots out there too. You'd bring a pretty good price."

"I think he plans to take us to Earth."

Paul was getting his confidence back. I knew that when he said, "Well, he'd better or he'll find himself in all kinds of trouble. I've taken enough nonsense from him."

I wanted to warn him not to get tough with Captain Becker, because the old space rat held all the cards. But

I didn't get a chance. We entered the lounge at that moment, and Captain Becker threw a crooked grin at Paul.

"How are your badges of honor coming, youngster?"

"My badges of honor?"

"Your calluses. The ones you're transferring from the seat of your pants to the palms of your hands."

If Captain Becker thought that would get a laugh from Paul, he was disappointed. Paul only frowned.

"I understand you want to talk business."

Becker didn't speak, and pretty soon Paul began to squirm a little.

"You did want to talk business, didn't you?" Paul asked hesitantly.

I guess Captain Becker didn't like a mere boy talking up to him the way Paul had, and wanted to make him less confident.

When he saw that he'd succeeded, he put on that twisted grin again.

"You want to get to Earth pretty bad, don't you?"

"We've got to get there."

"Things a person wants awful bad sometimes come high," Captain Becker said.

"First-class luxury fare is pretty high, isn't it?"

"I've been thinking maybe not high enough for the risk I'd be taking."

"I told you there won't be any risk. My father will pay you a reward."

"I've always been inclined to take the money at hand and not depend on what I might get later on."

"How much do you want?"

"Well, I've been figuring, and I think five thousand Earth dollars — just what you happen to have — might be about right."

"It's all I've got!" Paul yelped.

"But you can get more. Maybe your father will give *you* the reward for coming home."

"That's silly."

Captain Becker's face changed. It got very stern.

"I think you're right. I think we'll forget the whole thing and let the Marsport police decide what to do with you."

"They'll either destroy Rex or send him back to Ganymede!"

Captain Becker shrugged. "Your father can buy you another robot. They're easy to come by."

"Not robots like Rex. You like Rex. You gave him a color bulb. You wouldn't want him destroyed, would you?"

Paul was pleading now, and Captain Becker seemed to be pondering the point as he looked at me.

"The color bulb was nothing. I bought a box of junk for a dollar, and it happened to be in there. He's a good robot. It would be a shame to see him destroyed. He's got a good personality."

I said, "Thank you," because I had heard humans say that when someone complimented them. It must have sounded funny, coming from a robot.

"He's got a wonderful personality," Paul said eagerly. "Why don't you take the money and let us stay on the ship until you reach your Earth port of call?"

"Well, as a favor to you, son, I guess maybe I'll take the chance. I'm not a cruel man."

As Paul pushed the money at him I couldn't help thinking that maybe Captain Becker wasn't cruel, but he knew how to swing people around to where he wanted them. Paul had been angry when Captain Becker demanded a pirate's rate for our fare.

But now, after he'd changed his approach, Paul was forcing the money into his hands.

"I won't have to work any more, will I? First-class passengers aren't supposed to scrub floors."

Captain Becker laughed, and it was hard to tell whether it was a friendly laugh or not.

"I think we can find a few easier jobs for you. Young hands hadn't ought to be idle. That's what my daddy always taught me."

It was hard to imagine Captain Becker ever having had a father. He looked as though he'd been the way he was forever. But he was a human, and humans are all born very small and grow up. It must have happened to Captain Becker too.

Paul and I had more time after that. Captain Becker laid out some jobs for Paul, but didn't stay around to see that he did them, and Paul didn't work very hard.

We talked about what we would do when we got to Earth.

"The family was moved to the company's main office in Toledo," Paul said, "but there won't be any problem getting there from Kansas City. Transportation is very good on Earth."

"They have lots of skimmers?"

He laughed. "Yes, but we won't use one. We'll go by copter, probably. That's a kind of passenger plane, and it goes even faster than a skimmer. It will take us from the Kansas City spaceport to Toledo in about forty-five minutes."

"Earth must certainly be a wonderful place. I'm glad I've got a color bulb. I'll be able to see so much more."

"We could go by monorail too. A monorail is a big jet car that hangs from an overhead rail and goes almost as fast as a copter."

"Are there lots of robots on Earth?"

"That's where all robots are made. You came from Earth. Don't you remember any of it?"

"No. I remember when your father bought me for you. It was in a big showroom with a lot of models. But then I was deactivated and shipped to Ganymede by freight. Your father picked me up in Ganapolis."

"I've been thinking about something," Paul said.

"What?"

"There are a lot of batteries here on the *Terrabella*."

"That's right. Captain Becker has to keep a fairly big supply in case he can't find replacements on the outer planets."

"I think you ought to take an extra set as a reserve. There's room in your torso box to store them."

"But that would be stealing."

"Are you out of your mind? We're paying that bandit four fares already to get to the Earth! Don't you think he ought to throw in a couple of batteries?"

That put it in a different light. It made sense.

"All right. I'll charge a set of batteries and put them in my torso box in case I need them. I don't think we will."

"You never can tell," Paul said darkly.

And I didn't realize at the time how right he was.

As we approached Marsport, Captain Becker kept staying in his cabin more and more. He took the two-way radio I'd repaired, and I supposed he was picking up the music that comes in on the Interplanetary Services.

He came out of his cabin in plenty of time to pilot the *Terrabella* into Marsport, and I suggested to Paul that he'd better get back in his cabin while we were in port, so as not to take any chances of inspectors seeing him during the layover.

After I'd fixed his lock so his cabin looked unoccupied, I went into the pilot's cabin and watched Captain Becker bring the ship in.

He was sullen and didn't have anything to say, and I decided that he must have been scared. After all, he had a lot to lose if the authorities found out what he was doing. And I was glad Paul had had enough money to make him do it.

As we settled on our assigned ramp, he took off his earphones and turned to me. His expression was defiant.

"Bring the youngster here," he said.

"Isn't it better for him to stay in his cabin in case somebody boards the ship?"

"Nobody boards my ship unless I say so. Bring him up here."

I went and got Paul. We entered the pilot's cabin, wondering what Captain Becker had in mind.

We found out pretty quick.

He had a wad of Earth dollars in his hand. He thrust them at Paul.

"Here — take your money."

Bewildered, Paul put out his hand and closed it over the big roll of bills.

"You don't want it?"

"I may be a bit sharp. I may borrow a little. But I don't steal. Take your money. I don't want any part of it, and the deal's off. It's better for you, youngster. You shouldn't be learning bad habits at your age. You learn 'em, and they'll stick with you through life."

While we were wondering what all that meant, Captain Becker threw a lever on the control panel and got up from his chair.

By the time he got to the pilot's port it had opened.

Two hard-shelled Martian police walked in.

And all our long-range planning had failed.

11. Custody

THE TWO MARTIAN POLICEMEN were quick and business-like. "You are Captain Becker?" one of them asked. "Yes," the captain answered.

"We got a message from you about a runaway boy."

"This is the lad."

The other policeman took Paul by the arm, while the first one — carefully polite as all Martian officials are — bowed slightly to Captain Becker.

"You will have to come too, sir. Your report on this affair at the police station will have to be made in person."

Captain Becker shrugged with annoyance. "All right, if I have to, I have to. The boy stowed away at Ganapolis, and I found him fifteen days out of Marsport. That's all there is to it."

"The report must be made in person," the policeman insisted. "We will not take up much of your time."

"Stay here," Captain Becker said to me, and the three of them left with Paul, not even looking in my direction. After they were gone I stood there in the pilot's cabin trying to figure out what had happened.

Captain Becker had reported a stowaway, and the police had met us at the spaceport. That was easy to see. They had entered the *Terrabella* and taken Paul to the police station.

But why hadn't they taken me? I had been completely ignored.

It didn't make any sense.

I stood there going over it again and again.

I could understand why Paul had ignored me. He'd probably been as surprised as I was, but as long as they made no move in my direction he wasn't going to call me to their attention.

As I kept on thinking the situation over, another part of it got a little clearer. The Martian police either did not associate a boy stowaway on the *Terrabella* with the kidnaped governor's son on Ganymede, or else the kidnaping story hadn't been given any weight by Interplanetary Security.

That last seemed more likely to be true. Also, Captain Becker must have known the police weren't expecting a robot to be with Paul Simpson, or he wouldn't have dared to ignore me in his report.

It was all pretty confusing, and I decided all I could do was wait until Captain Becker came back and explained what had happened.

He was back in less than an hour. I hadn't moved. I was still in the pilot's cabin, and he came in and snorted at me as though daring me to object to what he'd done.

I didn't object, of course. A robot never objects to what a human does. But I did feel that I could ask some questions.

"Why did you turn Paul over to the police?"

"It was best for him. They'll send him home to his father."

"Why didn't they take me?"

He seemed to be deciding whether to answer or not. Then he said, "Why, you should consider yourself lucky that they didn't."

"But they wouldn't take Paul and leave me, his kidnaper, unless — "

"That kidnaping story was discounted," Captain Becker said. "The investigation back in Ganymede proved that Paul left the *Star Queen* of his own accord. There wasn't any robot with him. They couldn't find anybody who even remembered seeing you together. The police think you're stalled somewhere in the wild country on Ganymede with your batteries dead."

"Why didn't you tell them the truth?"

If Captain Becker fidgeted a little, his own guilt made him do it. And his own guilt made him explain himself to a robot. If he'd realized what he was doing, accounting to me for his actions, he would have shut me up in a hurry. But he didn't.

"It would have been harder to explain," he said. "The boy stowed away on my ship — that was the truth, and I couldn't do anything about it. But having a stolen robot with me would have been another matter. I did it the best way I could. I didn't lie. I just didn't tell all of it."

Captain Becker had a paper in his hand that he kept folding and unfolding. He laid it on a ledge and went on.

"It seems to me I was badly treated in this business, and I had a right to protect myself."

I was thinking what Paul had said — that robots brought good prices out where the Interplanetary Security didn't reach. Maybe that was what Captain Becker had in mind for me. Would I be worth a trip out there? Finally, I asked the question.

"What are you going to do with me?"

His look was peculiar. "I think I've got something coming out of this. I gave the boy his money back."

"What does that mean?"

"It means my two working robots aren't ready yet. It will take another month. If I turned you in, I'd be shorthanded."

"You're keeping me on the ship?"

"That's the idea. You stay aboard — under security while we're in a spaceport. You work the run to Earth, and then I'll take a load back to Ganymede and turn you over to that Mr. Hennings, the man you belong to."

Captain Becker rubbed his chin thoughtfully. "Maybe there'll be a reward for all my trouble after all. Hennings ought to pay a little something for getting a valuable property back. Bringing you back safe and sound when he thinks you're smashed up in a Ganymedian canyon somewhere ought to have a good psychological effect on him."

He stopped again as he kept on rubbing his chin. "Wonder if I ought to send a message to Hennings — no, guess I'll let it ride. No use giving him a chance to get impatient. Let him be surprised."

I could see that Captain Becker was feeling very guilty, because, even though I hadn't said a word, he suddenly looked at me and snorted. "It was for the boy's own good. I did him a favor, not mentioning you. He did steal you from Mr. Hennings. You can't get around that fact. This way, the police will probably never know that."

That was true, and there was nothing I could say. I'd been wondering what was on the paper Captain Becker had brought back, and I got a chance to find out when he left it where it was, on the ledge, and started to leave the cabin.

He stopped at the door. "You're to stay on board the *Terrabella*," he said, "and don't get any ideas about leaving. I put a time lock on the pilot's port so you can't open it. And I'll be watching the freight port. I'm going back and start the unloading. Come on with me."

He hurried out of the cabin, and before I followed him I grabbed the paper and read it. It said Paul had been put in custody of the mayor of Marsport. That surprised me at first, a runaway boy taken to the mayor's home.

But soon I realized that Paul was pretty important. He was the son of an important Earthman, Roger Simpson, an important official in one of Earth's biggest import and export companies.

That would make Paul special.

I went back into the cargo hold to help with the unloading. The three robots were at work, and Captain Becker was directing from outside the ship.

I wasn't thinking about escaping. There was no room

for any thought but the one that I would never see Paul again. It was over. We'd tried hard, but we'd failed. I decided it was probably better that way. Paul was growing up. Would he want a robot tagging around after him much longer?

He would be living on Earth, a place where he would find human friends. It had been different on Ganymede. There hadn't been any human children his own age around — none close enough to be his good friends. But all that would be changed on Earth.

Another thing: Ganymede was a rough, dangerous satellite. There, a boy needed a strong robot to protect him and keep him out of trouble. But he needed no such protection on Earth.

I got in line and began carrying crates out of the hold and piling them on the ground. And as I worked, I kept on thinking.

And kept on missing Paul.

Another thought came. What if Captain Becker had lied? All during the trip in from Ganymede he hadn't seemed very reliable. After finding Paul, he'd made a deal and had gone back on it. Maybe the story he'd told was not true. I couldn't think of any reason why it should not have been, but I was only a robot and robots are not supposed to be good thinkers. After bouncing all these thoughts around in my control box, I was sure of only one thing: I had to see Paul once more before we were separated forever — to get the truth, I told myself — even though I didn't really believe that. I knew it was just an excuse to be disobedient and go against the command of a human again, this time, Captain Becker.

109

I guess the idea for escaping must have formed earlier and was waiting to be used, because I didn't have to think it up. It was all ready.

I'd been carrying boxes, and the captain had been counting us as we went in and out of the hold. The next time I went into the hold I stayed there and began moving boxes forward toward the port from the main stack.

After a while Captain Becker came and peered inside. He watched me for a while and let me keep on doing it, figuring it would be easier to watch me if I stayed inside.

I was pretty sure that was how he would figure it.

As soon as he went away, I opened one of the crates and took the herb packs out. Then I gave the next robot an order.

"After the trip you're making now, take this crate out and put it on the back of the pile."

There was no reason for the robot to disobey the order, because it didn't cancel out the captain's basic order, to unload the hold.

After the robot left with the crate he was carrying, I got into the one I had emptied and pulled the top down into place. I waited. After a few minutes, the robot came back into the hold and picked the crate up and carried me outside.

He put me down and went back into the hold, and I adjusted my diaphragms to a very high pitch and waited. After a while I heard what I was listening for — Captain Becker's voice.

"Where did that robot go? Rex! Come back here and get to work!"

I raised the lid enough to clear the upper edge of my

110

refractor bulb and saw him disappear into the hold. He had looked in and found me gone.

Naturally he thought I'd gone into the forward part of the ship and was going up there to search.

I didn't waste any time. As he vanished around the edge of the lock into the ship, I climbed out of the box and went away from there.

Once clear of the Class 3 loading area, I felt a little better. There were a lot of robots of my type around, and I had a good chance of not being picked up for a while, even if Captain Becker had reported me as a runaway.

An even greater safety factor was Captain Becker himself. I didn't think he would make the report for a while. He'd try to find me himself first, because he would not have wanted the police to get interested in me. They would have asked for my serial number, which Mr. Hennings had no doubt given when he'd reported me as missing. The Martian police could have had that report in their files.

I had a good chance of evading pickup.

The Mars Complex is a pretty big place. A transfer point for traffic all over the System, it is in three sections. Marsport, where Captain Becker brought the *Terrabella* in, is for freighters only — a big, dirty, busy place where the sands of the Martian deserts sift in to get all over everything. Humans don't like it because the sand gets in their clothes. Robots don't like it because the sand gets in their joints. There are more robot-repair depots in Marsport than any other place in the System. And of course everybody wears the light Martian helmets — all humans, that

111

is — because the atmosphere is not dense enough to sustain human life, even though the heavier air suits of the outer planets and satellites aren't needed.

That's Marsport, but Mars City is something different. It's under a big plastic air bubble that took fifty years to build and needs a permanent crew of two hundred robots to keep it in repair. Mars City is twenty miles from Marsport, with a busy road connecting them.

The third part of the Complex is the big passenger spaceport called Marspoint — I suppose because it's the point where everybody comes and gets on another ship to go someplace else. The three units of the Complex are three points of a triangle, laid out the same way the colony was laid out on Ganymede.

That's what the Mars Complex consists of, and one of Paul's books said that over fifty per cent of all the people on Mars live in and near it.

The road from Marsport to Mars City is always thick with trucks and people and robots going back and forth. I trotted along with the others and was not in any great fear of being noticed.

I had a problem when I got to Mars City. I had to find out where the mayor lived.

I went in through an air lock, wondering how I was going to do this. I could get his address all right, and I did — from the visiphone book — but that didn't get me there. It listed the mayor under Government Officials and gave his address as 81 Redwine Place.

I didn't know where that was, and it could have been dangerous to ask, because robots are supposed to be out alone only when they are going on an errand. And when a robot runs an errand, he's supposed to know where he's going. I could have asked a robot, but that would have been a waste of time. Unless the one asked happened to be delivering a message or something to the mayor, it wouldn't know.

I went to what looked like the middle of the city and began looking at buses. There were lots of them going to all parts of the city, and I finally found one marked HILLSIDE AND REDWINE. When it started out, I trotted along, keeping it in sight and watching the street signs at the same time. After a while I found a street sign that said: REDWINE PLACE.

After that it was easy.

But then I faced up to my real problem, one I hadn't given any thought to: what I would do when I got there.

I could walk up to the door and ring the bell and ask to talk to Paul Simpson, but I didn't think they would let me. Robots do not go around asking to talk to humans unless they have a message for them, and in Mars City everybody used visiphones.

Maybe I wouldn't be able to see Paul. But I could perhaps find out about him.

I went back through a grove of trees and rang a bell at the back door of the house at 81 Redwine Place. It was built up on a hill, made mostly of glass, with drapes and shades inside. It was all on one level, the back door at the top of the hill so that you had to climb anyway if you were inside.

But I was outside, and after I waited a while a robot opened the door and asked, "What do you want?"

113

"I want to ask about an Earthboy you have here. Do you know about him?"

The robot, a domestic, did not question my purpose. "Yes, I know about him?"

"What do you know?"

"Nothing. I only know he was brought here."

"Can I see him?"

"No. I have no orders to let you in."

"How is the boy's health?"

"It is good."

"Where is he now?"

"He is in his room. He is asleep."

"Is he well taken care of?"

"He is well taken care of."

It was disappointing to come way out here and not see Paul after all. I should have done some long-range planning, I decided. But a robot can't know those things.

I wasn't getting anywhere with the domestic, so I said, "That was all I wanted to know," and turned away as the door closed.

No one seemed to be watching me. I stood there for a minute or two. I felt very sad. There didn't seem to be anything to do but to go back to Marsport and tell Captain Becker to put me under restraint again.

It was all working out for the best. I still had my earlier thoughts to fall back on — that Paul really didn't need me any more, and so it was better that I go back to Ganymede and work on Mr. Hennings' farm.

This was good safe thinking, because when a robot gets ideas about freedom and that sort of thing, it can only lead to trouble for him. I'd had a lot of good years with

Paul and I had my color bulb, which would give me a lot of pleasure until it burned out and Mr. Hennings replaced it with one for black and white. After he did that I could remember what color was like and get pleasure out of it that way.

I went around the corner of the house, heading back to the street I came in on.

And then I saw Paul.

He was inside of one of the glass-walled rooms. He had pulled the drape back and he was pounding on the glass, motioning to me.

I ran to the glass wall and put my diaphragm against it and heard him say, "This glass is too thick, Rex. I can't break it! Get me out of here!"

It was an order, and the glass was easy. I doubled my steel fist and hit it and it smashed. I hit it again, and there was a hole big enough for Paul to crawl through.

He came out with his helmet gripped in one hand and a big grin on his face.

"Rex! I knew you'd come. I was waiting!"

"What do we do now?"

"We hide. They'll be after us. You've got to find a place we can hide!"

"We'd better get away from here first."

We went the other way. Not toward the street, but back into the grove of trees behind the house. The trees did hide us, and as I looked back nobody had come to the smashed wall yet, but I was sure it wouldn't be long.

But going in that direction was a bad move. I should have noticed that the mayor lived very close to the wall of the air bubble over Mars City. When we got beyond the grove, we were right up against it. And out beyond, there was nothing but a flat expanse of Martian sand as far as you could see — open, flat stretches with no cover. There was no sense in breaking the bubble — a serious crime — and trying to escape in that direction.

"What will we do?" Paul said.

"I'll dig," I told him.

There was sand on the inside of the bubble too, and I dug hard and fast with both my arms. Before long I had a hole deep enough for both of us. We got in, and I pulled the sand in over us.

Paul had put his helmet on, and we lay in the hole so that the helmet touched my control box. That way, we could talk.

I couldn't level the sand out over all of us — only up to our shoulders. But I pulled my arms down and the sand fell in around them.

If anybody looked close, they would have seen us, but I was hoping nobody would. I hoped they would go in the other direction when they started searching. They wouldn't expect us to trap ourselves against the wall of the bubble and dig a hole to bury ourselves.

It would look like too stupid a thing to do.

12. The Wastelands

"**I** KNEW YOU'D FIND ME."

"I wouldn't have known where you were, but Captain Becker had a paper he brought back. I read it."

"I stayed at the police station only a little while. Boy, it's hot — buried in sand."

"If they don't find us, we'll have to stay under here for two or three hours — until it gets dark."

"There's sand sifting into my helmet."

"Try to lie very still."

"The mayor of Mars City told me I'd go back to Earth on the fastest, latest luxury liner. I think he wanted to get in good with Dad."

"Maybe it would be better if you went back."

"And leave you here? What are you talking about? Do you think we've gone through all this trouble just to quit now?"

"But I'm beginning to wonder if we can win."

"Rex! I never heard you talk that way before!"

"I never felt like this before. When I was leaving the house after they wouldn't let me see you, I decided it was best."

"I'll say what's best, Rex!"

"All right. But stay calm, or you'll get sand in you."

That was the way we talked while we were buried under the ground in the mayor's back yard. I knew they would be hunting for Paul, but I wasn't sure they'd know he had a robot with him. The domestic I'd met at the back door wouldn't say anything unless he was asked. They might think Paul had escaped by himself.

In that case they wouldn't be looking for us where we were. They wouldn't expect a boy to dig a hole in the sand and bury himself.

"How long have we been here?" Paul asked.

"About half an hour."

"Time goes slowly when you're buried, doesn't it?"

"We ought to decide what we're going to do when we get out of here."

"I've got my money back. We'll go to Marspoint and take a ship back to Earth."

"I suppose that's the smartest thing to do."

"The thing to do is to get home. Dad's objection to taking you in the first place was the cost. Once I get you there, he'll have to agree to let me keep you."

"There's one thing you forget — Mr. Hennings. The money you'll use for tickets comes out of what he paid for me. As Captain Becker said, I'm a stolen robot."

Paul thought that over. "The tickets will cost about half

the money I've got. That will leave half of it to send back to him."

"But I'm pretty sure Mr. Hennings will want all of it."

"Dad said he would buy me a new robot. Maybe he'd be willing to give me half of what a new one would cost, as long as I don't need a new one."

Paul spoke hopefully, and I wished that I could cheer him up by agreeing with him. But I couldn't.

"I think maybe your father expected you to use the money he gave you to buy a new one when you got to Earth."

Paul didn't have any answer to that.

"Another thing," I said, "Mr. Hennings might not be satisfied with getting his money back. I'm still legally his property. He might insist that I be sent back to Ganymede."

"It would cost him a lot in freight charges."

"I think the police would make your father pay the charges."

I heard Paul sigh. "We can't make things add up right, can we?"

"Sometimes it's very hard."

"Well, we'll worry about those problems when we have to face them. The thing to do is get home to Earth. That still goes. And I hope night comes before I bake clear through."

Night finally came, and we crawled out of the hole and looked around. We were all alone.

"We want the road to Marspoint," Paul said. "Do you know where it is?"

"It's got to be in that direction," I said. "We better go out of the bubble here and cut across the desert and hit the road away from the city. We're going to have to be awfully careful. They'll be looking for us. And they may know we're together."

"I think they'll figure we headed back to Marsport and the freighters."

It was as good a way to think as any, as long as we didn't know for sure one way or another. I didn't say anything, but I was going to be very careful.

I got down and began to dig. As I worked, Paul kept a lookout behind us, and when I'd dug out enough to get through, I had Paul crawl out under the edge of the bubble to the desert beyond. I followed him, pulling the sand back into the hole. It was plugged tight, and the city's air wouldn't escape.

We started toward the road and had the first of our bad luck — a sandstorm.

The sandstorms of Mars are famous throughout the whole System. They come without warning. You're walking along across the desert with visibility unlimited one minute, and staggering through a wall of howling sand the next.

When this happens in the daytime, it's bad enough. But when you're hit by a sandstorm at night, it can scare humans to death. They have been known to panic and choke to death on the sand after their helmets were knocked off.

When the sandstorm hit I grabbed for Paul to hold him close. But I was frightened, myself — because he wasn't there. He had been hit by a wall of stinging sand and driven away from me.

I circled desperately trying to find him. The howl of the storm blotted all sound out of my diaphragms, and it was possible that I would never find Paul — that I would miss him and that he would be buried by the time the storm was over.

I've heard that under such conditions, humans pray. I wanted to pray too, but I didn't know how. All I was able to do was repeat the words, "I've got to find him — I've got to find him — " over and over again.

And perhaps doing that is some kind of robot prayer, because I did find him. One of my outspread arms bumped into something. I grabbed, and it was Paul.

I felt and found that his helmet hadn't been knocked off. I put my control box against it and said, "It's all right. Don't be afraid. Stay inside the shelter of my arm."

"We're lost!" Paul said. "We can get lost in the desert and never find our way out. We'd better stand still and not move."

"We don't have to do that. I can tune in on the Marspoint radio beam and we'll follow it."

"I forgot that," Paul said.

Which shows that panic can make a human very unreliable. But not robots. A robot's faculties, even though they are limited, work automatically under any conditions that do not destroy their mechanism.

Holding Paul in the crook of my arm, I set my antenna on the Marspoint beam and began moving in that direction. But it was against the wind, and Paul couldn't move. I picked Paul up and carried him, and then we began making a little progress, although I sank ankle-deep in the sand at every step.

He put his helmet against my control box and said, "This is taking a lot of your charge."

"It's all right," I answered. "I've still got the batteries we took from the *Terrabella,* and the ones I'm using are almost full."

We plodded on.

The Marspoint beep came steady and clear into my receiver, and I was able to ride it in a fairly straight line except when I hit a pile of rock. But I got back on the beam beyond the rock pile without much trouble.

Once we almost fell into a gully. It wasn't too deep, and I crossed it without losing the beam.

After a while the storm let up, dying into a few swirls and snarls. When it was over, we could see Deimos and Phobos (I got their names out of one of Paul's books) racing across the Martian sky.

We stopped, and Paul shook as much of the sand out of his clothes as possible. He took off his helmet and emptied it, and when we were ready to go on we were both almost as good as new.

The beam had taken us off the road, and instead of returning to it, we kept on following the beam. Its beep brought us to the Marspoint bubble, and we held a conference before going around to the air lock.

"Maybe we ought to split up," I said.

"Why?" Paul asked. "They won't necessarily be looking for a boy and a robot together."

"Perhaps not, but Captain Becker is probably trying to get me back."

I explained to Paul why I thought the captain wouldn't tell the police I had escaped — that this would put him in the position of having to answer a lot of questions he wouldn't want brought up.

But he might have gone to some private detective agency and commissioned them to find me. There are several of these agencies doing business in the Mars Complex, because it's a big System transfer point — a place where runaways and people trying to escape from something are likely to turn up.

"If he's heard about your escaping from the mayor's home," I said, "he'll probably figure that we're together. They might be watching for us as a team."

Paul thought that over. "We've got to get two tickets somehow," he said. "Two on the next ship going out for Earth. You say they'll probably figure that we're spooking around the freighter over at Marsport, trying to stow away again. But they'll be smart enough to cover the Point, on the chance we might come here."

That was true, and I did some thinking myself. If they were watching, and Paul walked up to buy tickets, we'd be finished before we started.

"I ought to buy the tickets while you stay out of sight," I said.

Paul weighed that to see if it made sense. "I don't see why it shouldn't work."

"It ought to be less dangerous than the other way."

"It shouldn't surprise anybody — a robot buying space tickets. A lot of people must send their domestics to run errands like that."

"If I had a note, it would look even better."

"Yes," Paul said. "I wonder if I've got a paper and pen."

He was excited and all keyed up, or he wouldn't have had to paw around in his pockets. He would have known that he wasn't carrying equipment like that. Neither was I.

"I'll slip inside and get some memo paper and a pen off of one of the desks," I said. "You stay here. I'll be right back."

"All right," Paul said, "but hurry."

I didn't want him getting nervous and doing something foolish. I said, "I'll go as fast as I can, but don't get edgy if it takes a little while. I can't just lumber in and swipe a pen off a desk. They're chained to hooks in the plastic."

"You can break the chain."

"Yes, but I don't want an attendant to see me doing it. That might be the end. I'll have to wait until I'm sure nobody sees me."

I left Paul out in the shadows and went around to the air lock. A lot of people were coming and going, because there is never any letup in the activity at Marspoint. The ships jet in and blast off all through the Martian day and night. Traffic goes on endlessly. I went in with a lot of humans and robots and was not at all conspicuous.

The Marspoint bubble doesn't cover the whole Point. It's a comparatively small one over the ticket offices and restrooms and eating places and such, with tunnels running out to the boarding ports of the ships.

The place was filled with noise and color (which I wasn't quite used to yet) and activity. There were people and creatures from all over the System. The polite, green-shelled Martians always seemed to be apologizing for being alive. I saw three seven-foot, wall-eyed Venusians, their bodies pure white, sitting together eating fish out of a basket. Venusians live on a certain kind of fish they catch on their own planet. The fish are all that they can eat, so they always take their food with them in a basket wherever they go. I do not like the Venusians. They are very ugly.

There was also a party of Mercurians — maybe a dozen — their bodies much different from those of the Venusians or of any other of the System peoples. Small, dried-out, fireproof bodies. You can hit a Mercurian with a blow-torch, and if it was from the back he wouldn't even look around.

Most of the travelers were from Earth. Earthmen dominate the System. They were the first and only ones to make spaceships to go anywhere in the System.

Earthmen and Earthwomen are always self-confident and sure of themselves, and aren't liked very well by the peoples of the other planets and satellites. This always seemed strange to me, because the Earth people have done so much for everyone else. They made space travel possible and gave a lot of the people on other planets a better way of life. Therefore it would seem that the other peoples should be grateful and like the Earth people. But they don't.

That is one of the things about human nature that never made sense to me. But I'm only a robot, and robots aren't supposed to understand such things.

I'll say one thing for the Earth people. They don't let not being liked stop them. They go right on doing things for the System as though they were loved and cherished clear out into infinity.

But things like that weren't bothering me too much at the moment. I was more interested in snagging one of the pens and memo pads off the desk than anything else.

I stayed in the background and sidled around the wall toward the desks where people were writing out messages to be sent over the System. The tables weren't crowded at the time. One of them, back in a corner, was empty except for a Plutonian who was finishing his message. As I approached the desk, he wriggled his spidery antenna the way Plutonians keep doing and put down the pen and walked away.

I slipped into his place and picked up the pen. I covered the chain that fastened it to the desk with one arm and was about to jerk it loose when a quick, commanding voice said, "Put the pen down, robot. Come with me."

I turned and got the human in the range of my refractor bulb. He was an Earthman, but there was nothing official-looking about him. A short, cold-faced man with a grim mouth and a definite manner.

He could be only one thing, I was sure: a private detective.

Resistance was out of the question. A robot, unless he is abnormally adjusted, does not become hostile to a human. Of course I could have been conditioned against obeying him by a previous command, but in that case I would have frozen — just stood there giving no response at all.

It all depended on my circuits. Some robots, handled carelessly, are easily stolen. Others would have to be moved with a block and tackle.

In my case, I tried to think. I didn't want attention

called to myself, so the logical thing was to go with the man. If I was being stolen, I would have plenty of time to freeze later. But I was pretty sure what had happened. The long arm of Captain Becker had reached out, and I had no plans about what I could do.

The only answer seemed to be — nothing.

I went with the detective to a small room on the far side of the big depot. He opened the door, and I went in and stood waiting.

There wasn't much in the room. A desk and two chairs and a sign on the wall that read: INTERSPACE DETECTIVE AGENCY.

There was another man sitting at the desk, and neither of them looked as though they liked their jobs very well, but maybe they did.

The man at the desk looked up, inquiring silently with his expression, and the man who had brought me in said, "This one was alone. He was at a desk getting ready to write something."

The other man looked me over critically and consulted a paper on his desk.

"Model's right. Type's correct. You say he was writing?"

"He was getting ready to."

"That fits the intelligence capacity."

In a kind of stupid gesture of defense, I was holding my arm over the serial-number plate on my torso box. It wasn't going to help. All they had to do was to tell me to move my arm.

But just as the man at the desk was about to do this so that he could make a final identification check, a third man jerked the door open and gestured violently.

The other two detectives alerted themselves immediately and hurried out of the room after him — but one of them stopped to lock the door from the outside.

I thought about quite a few things while I stood there waiting for them to come back. I could break the door open and run for it. If I did that I'd be stopped halfway across the depot, because a robot doesn't smash his way through a door without being noticed.

I could probably have gone the other way — through the wall of the room and out the other side. But that was risky too. No doubt whoever might be out there would think there was something unusual about a robot knocking a wall down and coming through.

I stood there, and I was pretty sure it was the finish. Regardless of how it worked out, I was going to end up back on Ganymede and Paul would go back to Earth alone.

It seemed all wrong. We'd broken a lot of rules — that was true. But we had tried so hard. And all we wanted was to be together. Was that too much to ask?

Then I began looking at it sensibly. It would be better for Paul. He'd gone to a lot of trouble to keep me with him, but now it was all over. He would go back to Earth and make new friends and forget me.

Or his father would buy him another robot.

That last thought made me feel very sad. I didn't mind the new friends. In fact, I was glad about that. But Paul having another robot! I guess that hurt me as much as it is possible for a robot to be hurt. But probably that isn't very much, with a robot's limited capacities.

As I stood there, I remembered one of the books Paul had read to me. It said that if you try hard enough to get a thing you will succeed, because nothing can stand in the way of supreme effort.

But either the human who'd written the book hadn't known what he was talking about, or our effort hadn't been supreme enough.

But that didn't matter much one way or the other.

After a while the door opened and the two detectives came back into the room. They picked up where they'd left off. I dropped my arm and the desk man read my number and compared it with the one on the paper.

He shook his head. "Wrong guess," he said. "Marko's runaway was a different series."

Evidently they were looking for the runaway robot of a man named Marko.

The man who had brought me in looked disappointed. "O.K.," he said, "back to the grind."

"Send this robot on his way," the desk man said. "His owner will be looking for him. No reason to start explaining if we don't have to."

The other man opened the door and looked at me. He said, "Go back where you were, robot. Go on with what you were doing."

I went back to the desk and stole a pen and a memo pad and took them out to Paul.

He was very nervous. "It took a long time," he said. "Did you go to sleep?"

"No, but the place was very crowded. There were a lot of people around the desks, I had to wait."

I saw no reason why I should upset him by telling what had happened, as long as it had turned out all right.

I lay down on the ground, and Paul used my torso box for a desk while he wrote a note on the memo pad.

It told the ticket seller to give the bearer two first-class tickets to the Toledo spaceport on Earth, and to assign him two reservations on the next jet out.

Paul showed it to me, and I couldn't see anything wrong with it.

"Go in and get the tickets," he said. "I'll wait here. If we get a break, we'll be in a cabin on an Earth-bound jet before it's daylight."

I went back into the depot and got in the ticket line. When I got to the window, I handed the ticket seller the note along with some money Paul had given me. The ticket seller was a Martian who had treated his shell to make it bright green. This is a prestige symbol among the Martians, although I've never been able to figure out why.

But I didn't care. His shell could be purple with orange spots, if only he would give me the tickets.

He did. He punched them out and made the change and gave it back to me with the tickets. Then he looked at the reservation visiboard.

"The *Oklahoma*," he said. "Ramp 7. It jets at 21:06. Forty-five minutes to board."

He made a note of that on a piece of paper and gave it to me and said, "Next, please."

I took the note and the tickets back to Paul outside. He grinned and breathed a big sigh I could hear on my diaphragms.

"We made it, Rex. Forty-five minutes to board. We're practically on our way to Earth."

We were not on our way to Earth yet, as far as I could see. It was still a long way to that cabin. But things did look better, and I didn't want to sadden Paul or make him feel bad.

"Almost on our way. That's what comes of good long-range planning," I said.

"There's no reason why we can't go inside and wait, is there? We'll have to go in anyway before long. We can stay apart, and maybe I can grab a sandwich. I'm hungry."

I followed behind Paul and found a place out of the stream of traffic where I could watch as he went to the refreshment counter and ordered something to eat. As far as I could see, no one was paying any attention to him. A single boy was easily overlooked in the crowded depot, because there were quite a few of them.

Near where I was standing there was a family waiting to board a jet — a mother and a father with an older daughter and a small son. A shiny new robot, evidently belonging to them, stood nearby.

The boy was crying. "But I want Jimmy on the ship with me!" He cried. "It's not fair! You said he could come."

The father was trying to quiet him down. "I know, Arthur. And I thought he could. But I'm trying to tell you — there's a rule, and I just found out about it. It's posted right there on the wall. There's nothing I can do."

The boy kept on crying, and the father turned to the mother. "Why don't you take him and buy him something — a cold drink, maybe? Take his mind off it."

"All right."

She went away with the boy and the girl. The father turned to the robot.

He said, "Come on, Jimmy. We'll see what's to be done about you."

They went off together and I went to where that sign was posted on the wall. I read it. It said:

Positively no robots allowed on passenger jets. Robots must be shipped separately from the Marsport freight dispatch office. Shipping priority for one robot — not over fifteen hundred pounds — is extended with every two first-class jet tickets. Overweight up to two thousand pounds accepted on an extra-charge basis. Shipper must assume responsibilty of presenting robot at dispatch office at Marsport.

That was it. We'd won only to lose. It seemed that the spaceways had too many tricky rules for a boy and a robot to outguess. Everywhere we turned, they had us stopped. Now we would have to start all over again.

13. Separate Trails

W E WOULD HAVE TO START ALL OVER AGAIN because complying with the spaceway rules would have been impossible. We couldn't get on the passenger jet together. That would have been impossible. Paul couldn't present me for shipment at the Marsport freight station without having to answer a lot of routine questions he'd be unable to give satisfactory answers to. And I couldn't go alone, because a robot can't ship himself.

I kept on thinking about it, and I decided Paul might be able to present me for shipping and get away with it. It had seemed impossible at first, but he could say he represented his father. And after all, he wasn't a child. He was sixteen years old.

But could he possibly avoid recapture?

Then a plan shaped up. Paul could present me for shipment. I would land on a freighter bound for Earth. That way, I'd be out of sight. He could deliberately let himself get picked up, and the authorities would see that he got back to his father.

It was a pretty good plan, and it made me feel good. I stood there watching Paul at the refreshment counter, and another thought came into my mind. This was all wrong. Paul had done a lot for me. He'd rebelled and broken a lot of rules to keep me with him. His father would be angry with him, and before we succeeded in what we'd set out to do he could still get into a lot more trouble.

I thought my plan was a good one, but we'd tried one good plan after another and they had all gone wrong.

It wasn't right. Paul belonged back on Earth with his father. And I belonged on Ganymede — on Mr. Hennings' farm. That was the way it had to be.

But to make it work out that way, I had to come up with another plan. Paul would never agree that we should give up. If I told him how I felt, he would give me an order and I would have to obey, and things would probably go from bad to worse.

I stayed where I was and watched him finish his sandwich. Nobody paid any attention as he left the refreshment counter and came toward me. He leaned carelessly against the wall nearby and didn't look at me.

"It's about time to board," he said. "We'll have to do that together."

"Do you think we'll be questioned at the port?"

"It's possible. But we've got to take the chance."

"Maybe we can fix it so they won't have a chance to do any questioning until the port is closed and locked. Then it will be too late."

"How could we fix that?"

"We hold our own tickets. We wait until a couple of minutes before the lock closes on the countdown schedule. You hurry up the ramp with your ticket and say, 'My robot's coming in a minute.' Then you rush on into the ship so they can't ask any questions. I'll wait until the very last moment. I'll time it very carefully and run up the ramp and give them my ticket and say, 'I'm with the boy who just boarded.' I'll hurry on in too, and the port will close behind me and they can ask all the questions they want. It will be too late for them to put us off."

"I think it's a very good idea." Paul looked at me curiously. "It's the best idea you've ever had. Too good for a robot, don't you think?"

"Yes, but probably something you said to me suggested it."

"I suppose that's what happened."

We crossed the depot toward the loading ramps, being careful not to get too close together. I watched Paul go in and start climbing the ramp, and I went to a window beside the entrance where I could see him present his ticket to the uniformed Earthgirl at the port. He said something, and the girl frowned and replied. I knew what her answer was. When he'd said his robot would be along, she'd told him robots were not allowed on passenger jets.

Paul glared at her. He was angry and confused. But he went on inside, and the port lock was swinging into locking position. It was too late for him to get off.

He was on the ship bound for Earth, where he belonged. And I was in the depot, where I belonged, ready to be delivered by Captain Becker back to Ganymede.

I had tricked Paul into going onto the ship by fooling about the time. I'd told him when to move, and he'd taken my word that it was right because I can measure time spans to the exact second in my control box.

It was over. I'd betrayed Paul and proved myself to be an unreliable robot. He would probably never forgive me. That was all right. We would never see each other again. If he thought ill of me, he probably wouldn't be so lonesome.

After the *Oklahoma* jetted off, I left the place where I was standing and started to leave the bubble. I didn't have to be very smart to figure my next step. Back to Marsport. Back to the clumsy old *Terrabella*. Back to Captain Becker — and Ganymede.

There was a very sad incident as I was leaving the depot. A sudden yell went up inside. "Mad robot! Mad robot!"

I was a little way outside the entrance, and I turned to watch with the rest of the crowd. A few moments later the wall of the bubble went to pieces in a big crash, and a robot came charging out.

He was my make and model, but a lot different inside. His control box had gone bad in one of those strange ways that humans have never been able to do anything about. They have every possible safeguard built into us. But our electronic equipment is so delicate and so finely balanced that once in a while it goes out of line without throwing any of the safety switches that render a robot immobile in ninety-nine out of a hundred cases.

The one we were watching was the hundredth case.

The robot charged in a straight line, ready to destroy anything in his path.

The guards in the depot had been caught napping and hadn't gotten the ray guns out in time. A man in plain clothes, probably a private detective, fired at the berserk robot several times. He had a small gun, and the slugs bounced off the robot's steel surface.

The robot ran in a straight line across the road and out into the desert and the shadows of night. He knocked down three humans on the way: a female, who screamed and clutched at her leg where the robot trampled her; a male, who went down and cracked his skull against the cement of the roadway and lay still; the third, a male who was foolish enough to try to stop the robot with his bare hands. The robot grasped him by the throat with one steel claw and threw him like a piece of refuse. The man went end over end and landed in a writhing heap by the roadside.

When four uniformed guards came out with ray guns, the robot was beyond range.

The immediate excitement over, I thought of my own safety. What if they started grabbing every unattached robot in the place? There had been cases of other robots responding sympathetically to their own kind and going berserk as a result of seeing the madness.

I decided it was best to get out of there. So I left the road and headed off into the desert in the opposite direction. I planned to get several miles away from Marspoint, out into the empty desert, and then set my receiver on the Marsport beam and get back to the *Terrabella*. I ran because I wanted to make it before daylight if possible.

Everything went all right for a while. Nobody tried to stop me. I heard sounds of activity out in the desert and from the direction of Marspoint, but none of it came close to me.

I was doing fine. I had put five miles between me and Marspoint, and was ready to beam in on the Marsport signal when a figure reared up in the desert ahead of me and let go with a ray gun.

I loosened the joints of my legs and dropped to the ground just in time to keep my control box from being melted off.

There was a gully about twenty feet from me, and my self-preservation quotients were working perfectly, because I began rolling when I hit the ground and I was in the gully before the second shot was fired.

I heard the hunter — whoever he was — yell over his radio, "I got your radio message, and I've got your mad robot. I just chased him into a gully about four miles northwest of Marspoint. I don't think I hit him."

But by that time I wasn't in that gully any more. Moving low and fast, I went in the direction opposite from the man with the ray gun and found my way out at the far end.

"I'm going to move in on him," the man reported. "I'm well armed. I'll probably have him by the time you get here."

Not if I could help it, he wouldn't. But maybe I wouldn't be able to help it.

I could see what had happened. The guards, trying to

chase down the mad robot at Marspoint, had broadcast details and warnings.

The signal had been picked up by the man who was after me, and he had taken his ray gun and gone hunting. I thought he could have shown a little more restraint. Why didn't he find out whom he was shooting at before he let go? But he was out for the reward that is automatically paid for stopping a mad robot.

There were points in the man's favor. Any robot wandering in the desert at that time of the morning didn't make much sense. I would have been under suspicion in any case. He took it for granted I was the one from Marspoint.

It was still quite dark, and he probably hadn't seen me roll into the gully on purpose. A mad robot doesn't hide. He must have thought I'd turned in that direction by accident.

But I was trying to keep accidents from happening — especially accidents with a ray gun. I wasn't doing anything by chance.

When I got to the end of the gully, I stopped a minute and hunted for Marspoint wavelength on my receiver. The ray gunner was getting information, and I saw no reason why I shouldn't have it too. I found the wavelength and a voice came in.

"The robot must have circled. He's highly dangerous. We advise caution. Keep him in sight, but don't engage him until help arrives."

"I said I was well armed," the gunner replied. He sounded angry, and I thought I knew why. If the guards got there and they all began taking potshots at me, it would be hard to prove who fired the fatal ray and deserved the reward.

"Your gun might jam, and you'd be at his mercy."

The man answered that by saying, "I take care of my arms. They don't jam."

Personally, I hoped there wouldn't be any reward to argue about. I backed away as quietly as possible, straining my diaphragms and my refractor bulb in the direction of the gully.

The gunner was probably searching there by now. He would soon know I had kept on moving and would be after me.

I had one big problem: I couldn't get the Marsport beam and the Marspoint voices at the same time. I had to choose one or the other.

I decided the best thing to do was to get the Marsport beam. Otherwise I'd be floundering around in the desert and would be almost sure of getting picked off. So I took the beam and let the voices go. It came in clear and sharp with its fast-beat rhythm, and I began following it.

The beam led me at an angle that would cause me to pass the gully about three hundred yards to the south. I gave it a little more leeway by leaving the beam and adding another hundred yards to that distance at the point where I'd been shot at.

I couldn't hear anything from that direction, but in the soft Martian sand a man can be very quiet if he's stalking a nice reward.

I tried to be quiet myself and I got a little scared — as scared as a robot can get — when I realized I had only about half an hour more of darkness. If I got caught out there in daylight, I was a gone robot.

I began to run.

It's very hard to run and listen at the same time, but I didn't have any trouble hearing the next sizzling explosion of the ray gun.

I dropped instantly, crawled a few feet and hunted for cover. But there wasn't any this time. No friendly gully to fall into. I got up and began running again, expecting my control box to be melted down to a cinder at any moment.

The direction of the second shot told me a second gunner was out after the reward. It had come from my right and well ahead of me — a point the first gunner could not have reached so quickly.

I'd lost the Marsport beam, so I tuned in the communication wavelength to see what was going on. Everybody was talking at once. Marspoint kept saying, "Exercise caution — exercise caution. We're on the way."

The two close gunners had met up on the wavelength and were discussing the best way to trap me. While I ran and listened, I heard them agree to split the reward if they could get me before the patrol men got there.

It was strange, hearing myself being split up that way. But it didn't bother me any. If they collected the reward, I wouldn't be in a position to care who got it.

Suddenly I had a thought — something I could do to stretch the odds in my direction a little bit. I stopped running and crouched down and used the radio beam myself.

I yelled, "Help! Help! Mad robot! Mad robot!"

The patrol came in almost loud enough to break my transistors. "Where are you? Give us a location!"

"About six miles southeast of Marspoint. Hurry up. The robot just killed my grandfather and my uncle, and he's chasing my crippled brother."

I thought afterward that I might have laid it on a little thick, but nobody seemed to notice. Patrol yelled, "Are you armed?"

"I had a short club, but I lost it."

They groaned and replied, "Do the best you can. We're on the way."

That took the patrol off my neck, but I still had my immediate danger to contend with. The two gunners were yakking it up, as Paul would have said. They were confused.

"Do you suppose there are two of them on the loose?"

"I don't know anything about southeast," the other one said grimly, "but I know that what I saw charging across the sand wasn't a shadow. It was a berserk robot. That man the other side of Marspoint must be seeing ghosts."

"Ghosts don't kill your whole family," the other gunner said doubtfully.

I was using the time to get away from there. I circled wide, and then took a chance and tuned in the Marsport beam again. It wasn't there, so I tried to estimate my position and moved off to my left.

I found it about five hundred yards in that direction and altered my course.

"There he is!" one of the gunners yelled.

I didn't need a radio to hear him. His voice came faintly from over my right shoulder.

I looked back in fright. But then I heard the other gunner's voice. "Watch it, you idiot! This is me!" There had been a hot, sizzling sound and the man yelled, "Put that gun down! You want to fry me?"

I heard a mumbled apology. I began running hard, thinking that their confusion might hold them for a while.

Dawn was beginning to break, and I risked an even greater effort at running. The way a robot is built, it can rise from any prone position it goes into by itself, from a squat or a crouch. But if it falls accidentally, it can go into a position of helplessness and require aid to rise again.

That was what I had to be careful of. But I had to be careful about getting my control box melted too, so a certain risk was necessary.

I plowed on through the sand and took a lot of chances. Dawn flared up. Finally I had a little luck, because before long I could see the road that led into Marsport. I could see the big ships in their freight berths, and men and robots moving around, busy with loading and unloading.

I slowed to a walk and got onto the road without attracting attention. From that point, it was easy. As I walked toward the *Terrabella*'s berth, I hoped they had stopped the mad robot. It would be for his own good as well as that of the humans.

A mad robot can never be happy. He wants to die.

The *Terrabella*'s ports were closed, and there was no activity in her berth. I went up the ramp and knocked on the pilot port and pretty soon it opened.

Captain Becker peered out at me. "Well," he snorted, "the return of the prodigal son. Where have you been?"

"A lot of places. But I want to come back now."

"Oh, you do! Just like that. Have you been out trying to find Paul?"

"Yes."

"He got away from you. He smashed the wall at the mayor's house and ran away. They're still looking for him."

Being around Paul so long — having him explain things to me — must have helped me a lot, because I could do elemental reasoning very easily. I knew right away why Captain Becker didn't ask me where Paul was, why he took it for granted that I didn't know. He assumed that if I'd found him I wouldn't have come back to the *Terrabella* alone. I probably wouldn't have come back at all.

"I failed," I said.

Which wasn't a lie.

I wasn't sure whether he was going to let me in. He stood in the port, squinting at me, trying to make up his mind about something and get the sleep out of his brain at the same time.

"Why aren't you loading?" I asked.

"Cargo's late. It'll be here this morning."

"Then you'll need help."

"You mean you're willing to go back to Ganymede?"

"Where else can I go?"

"That's very sensible. Too sensible. It makes me suspicious."

"If I wasn't willing to go back, I wouldn't have come here in the first place, would I?"

"I don't like robots parading their intelligence," Captain Becker snorted. He was in a bad mood, and I couldn't blame him.

"I'm sorry. But you will need help."

"I suppose you need a charge."

"I could use one."

He drew back from the doorway. "I'll decide what to do later."

"After the loading is finished," I thought.

"In the meantime go get your charge while I have breakfast. There'll be work to do."

I was glad he let me charge my own batteries. That way I could still hide the full ones I was carrying for emergencies.

I was pretty hungry, and took a full charge into my old ones. By that time Captain Becker had eaten and the cargo had been dollied in.

We went to work, and as we worked I thought of Paul rocketing toward Earth on the *Oklahoma*. It made me sad.

All morning I kept watching for the Marsport patrol to arrive. But nobody came.

14. A Robot's Lot

SOMETIMES THERE ARE THINGS I REMEMBER from books
Paul read me that describe the way real-life affairs
turn out. There was one that described what happened
after I got back to the *Terrabella.*

I went into a backwash.

That means a time when nothing much happens, a
waiting time until things get around to happening again.
Backwashes usually come when you expect a lot of
activity. At least that's when they seem to confuse you
the most.

I expected the police patrol to find their way to the
Terrabella eventually and start asking questions. They
didn't. I heard on Captain Becker's radio that the mad
robot had been caught and destroyed, and I supposed
they'd decided there was only one mad robot — not two.

146

No one showed up at the ship.

I also expected Captain Becker to ask me a lot of searching questions when he got around to it. But he didn't.

We loaded the ship — it took two days — and then got clearance for take-off to Earth. We lifted out of our berth on the morning of the third day after I got back, and while Captain Becker did pilot chores — clearing the ship, plotting his course, and setting the automatics — I cooked him a fine breakfast, taking some very rare recipes out of my memory bank.

My idea was to please him and put him in a good humor for the trip. He was in a good humor all right, or seemed to be, but I got a feeling that the breakfast didn't have anything to do with it.

After he'd eaten he didn't say a word about what had happened on Mars. It was as though he'd forgotten Paul ever existed. But he didn't forget to put me to work.

"The air-purifying system isn't working so well," he said. "Why don't you have a look at it? There are some guide manuals in the supply cabin if you want to check the circuit layouts."

That sounded all right, because I would just as soon have been working as not. I couldn't find the manuals, and had to go to his cabin to ask him where they were. He fumed because I woke him up from a nap, but he went to the supply cabin and found them for me.

I took them, and as I was leaving he got interested in some other books he found. That was how I left him — hunched over a box in the supply cabin, reading.

The air-purifying system wasn't broken, but it was dirty. I cleaned it out, changed the charcoal filters, and stepped up the oxygen generator, the work taking about three hours.

When I reported back to Captain Becker's cabin, he looked up from a book he was reading.

"How would you like to meet your father and mother?"

I thought maybe something had happened to his mind. "I never had a father and a mother. I — "

"Oh yes you did. You were manufactured at Glenwood Electronics on Earth, weren't you?"

"Yes."

"Then I can introduce you to your father and your mother. In fact, I can show you exactly how you were born."

He motioned, and I walked to his chair and looked at the book he was reading.

"I found this in the supply cabin," he said. "Don't have the least idea where it came from. It's all about robot manufacture — complete with diagrams and pictures. It was put out by the Glenwood people."

He held up the book so I could see one of the pages. It was a photograph of a room. There were electronic instruments on benches and big cabinet-enclosed power units. It was a clean room — everything white and polished and spotless.

There were a man and a woman in the photograph. The woman was young and smiling. She was very beautiful by Earth standards and wore a clean white coat.

"That's the activating laboratory at Glenwood," Captain Becker said. "So the girl is your mother and the man is your father. You came to life in that room."

The man had a thin, intense-looking face. He didn't look

anything like Paul's father. I guess I thought all fathers should look like Roger Simpson.

Captain Becker put the book down. He was squinting at me with a thoughtful expression on his face.

"How does it feel to be a robot?"

I couldn't think of any words to answer him with. "I don't know."

"A man alone thinks a lot," he said. "Out on the spaceways there's more time. I've got my music, but when that begins to bore me I ponder any number of things. And I've wondered a lot about robots."

"I've wondered a lot about humans."

He laughed. "Do you feel inferior to humans?"

"I guess so. Inferior means less, doesn't it?"

"It means not up to the level of someone else. Not as capable."

"I know I'm not as capable as a human."

"Does it bother you?"

"It makes me sad, I think."

"Then emotions must be of electronic origin."

"I don't think so. If they were, I'd be human."

"You may not be human, but you're a very exceptional robot."

"I am?"

"Compare yourself with my three loading robots."

"But their circuits are less complex than mine."

"Then creating a human robot is just a matter of inventing a complex enough circuit?"

I couldn't tell whether he was making fun of me or not. He seemed serious enough. It really didn't make any difference. I had to answer any questions he asked to the best of my ability. I'd been built with an obedience circuit that demanded this.

"I don't know, but I think it would be impossible for a robot to be a human. A human has to be born."

"But you're more intelligent than some humans."

"Then they would have to be defective. Humans do become defective. They get sick."

He kept staring at me. It was a little like the long talks Paul and I had on Ganymede, only Paul was not interested in the same things.

"I think maybe man will outsmart himself someday," Captain Becker said. "Someday he'll build a robot so smart it will take over the universe and make men do the work."

"Men who did that wouldn't be very wise."

"A lot of them aren't, Rex. They're smart and clever and inventive. But not many are wise."

"There's a difference?"

"A big difference."

The conversation was beginning to bore him. He yawned. "I wish you could play chess," he said.

"I can."

His eyes brightened. "Is that a fact?"

"Paul taught me. After that I got a chess book and transferred it to my memory bank."

"That's fine. Get the chess set out of my cabin locker, and we'll separate the men from the robots. I'll show you the difference."

I got the set and laid the men out, and he made the first move. I countered it.

He moved again and I countered that. His next move

took almost a minute, and when he did move I made my countermove and waited again.

He looked up at me, irritated. "You don't have to move that fast."

"I didn't see any point in waiting. If you want me to move slowly, you must specify the waiting time. How long do you want me to wait between each move?"

"Oh, shut up," he snorted, and concentrated on the board.

When he moved, I countered immediately, since he hadn't ordered me to wait. Then I said, "I checkmate you in three moves. Black should now retire."

He was the black, and he didn't want to retire. He made the moves, and I checkmated him in three.

"Just luck," he said. "Just plain luck. You were just pushing pieces. You didn't have the least idea what you were doing. It's the last game you'll win on the whole trip!"

We set the men up again and started the second game. He was even slower now, studying each move. And he got madder and madder every time I moved without hesitation.

While he was thinking about his next move, I wondered why he took so much time. There is always only one right move in chess, and it's always so obvious anyone should be able to see it instantly.

When I beat him the second game, his face got red and I thought he was going to throw the board at me.

"You think you're pretty smart, don't you?"

"It's only memory," I said. "I put a lot of things about chess in my memory bank."

"You and your memory bank!"

"I know four hundred and eighty games — that's how many there were in the book. And I know eleven thousand, two hundred and twenty-four moves."

He dropped his hands in despair. "Great spaceways! What chance has a man got? I don't think men *might* create a robot to take over the universe. I think they've already done it." He knocked the board to the floor. "Get back to work."

I stood up. "What do you want me to do?"

"I don't care. Scrub the floor. Redesign the ship. Go build yourself a robot to scratch your back for you. Just get out of my sight."

I left the cabin, having arrived at a conclusion: Captain Becker was a poor loser.

I didn't redesign the ship, because that wasn't within my capabilities. Besides, the *Terrabella* was doing all right as she was, plowing down the spaceway toward Earth and not bothering anybody.

I didn't build a robot either, but I did scrub the companionway. I scrubbed it from one end to the other five times before Captain Becker got over his temper to a point where he was willing to speak to me. I think his appetite had something to do with it.

He came out of his cabin and looked at me. "Well, how long do I have to wait for dinner? What are you trying to do — put a hole through that planking?"

I got up and emptied my pails and got dinner.

After he'd eaten he was willing to talk, but his mood

hadn't improved much. "You're reconciled to going back to Ganymede. Is that right?"

"What is reconciled?"

"You're ready to go back."

It was a new word for me. "There isn't any place else to go."

"You're sure this isn't a trick? I've got a hunch you'll try to escape when we reach the Kansas City spaceport."

"You can prevent that."

"And I'm going to. I'm going to chain you up. I've had enough nonsense on this trip. First with you and the boy. Then you roam all over Mars and come back when you please. That's not going to happen on Earth."

He hadn't asked a question that I had to answer, so I didn't say anything.

He seemed a little sorry for having been so harsh, and after a snort or two he said, "Are you interested in what happened to Paul?"

"Yes."

"Nobody seems to know for sure. The case is getting some publicity. Nobody knows what happened to the lad after he left the mayor's house where he was being held in custody. His parents are worried. They're afraid he's wandering around on Mars somewhere."

"What do they think his reason is for not going home? He's got money, and he's old enough to find his way."

"They think he's mad at his father for taking you away from him."

"What does his father think about that?"

Captain Becker shrugged. He was watching me keenly.

"Who knows? I suppose he just wants his son back."

I got the feeling Captain Becker thought I knew more about Paul than I was telling him. Why didn't he ask me right out? Maybe, I thought, because he really didn't want to know. He'd had a lot of trouble with both of us, and if anything happened he wanted to be able to deny knowledge of all that had gone on.

I wondered whether I ought to tell him where Paul was. He could send a message to Paul's parents and they wouldn't be worried.

But I didn't tell him at that time. I wanted to think it over to make sure it was the right thing to do.

"Would you like to play some more chess?" I asked.

He scowled at me, and I went back into the galley and began cleaning up the dishes.

I had a lot of time to spend by myself, and I used it to look out at the stars and think. I never got tired of thinking. I know a lot of humans do, but a robot never needs sleep and probably doesn't think nearly as hard as a human, so he doesn't get tired.

I spent most of my time wondering what would happen when we got to Earth. By that time Paul would be back with his parents in Toledo. I would be chained in the *Terrabella* in Kansas City, so it wouldn't make much difference to me where Paul was.

But I knew that it did. It made a lot of difference. Paul was heading home and would certainly get there.

Suppose he didn't? What if he got lost? It wasn't logical, but I was only a robot. How could I be sure it wouldn't happen?

At the time I didn't have any idea of running away from Captain Becker. I'd decided to go back to Ganymede. Still, I didn't want to be helpless — chained in the ship — in case of something coming up that I couldn't foresee.

I decided to do something about that. What I had in mind was called a precaution — what Paul always called a "just-in-case."

I went to see about it.

15. The Blue Planet

I WASN'T SURE I COULD DO what I'd thought of, but it wouldn't hurt to try. It would take an advanced skill that I'd practiced only while Paul was growing up and learning to read and write. I knew the fundamentals, and I'd had machine-shop techniques that I'd used when Paul built model rocket ships and skimmers.

I thought that duplicating a robot's serial number was worth a try.

I didn't think much about the honesty of it. I guess at this stage I didn't care much about that. I'd never heard of a rule that said it was wrong for a robot to duplicate a serial number and I let it go at that. I'm pretty sure they never made the rule because they didn't think it was necessary.

I used the time Captain Becker spent in his cabin listening to his music to practice my penmanship in the machine shop. After a while I got pretty good at it.

I cut a small copper plate the exact size of the plate on the torso boxes of all robots. The original number is cut into the battery change and repair door, and it can't be removed, but a duplicate plate could be screwed over the original.

First, I picked one of the other robots — the cleanest one, with no identifying scratches or dents on him — and I copied his serial number. I took my time cutting it into the duplicate plate, working carefully and slowly until it was perfect.

When I came to my own, I had practice, so I finished it quickly.

Now I had two duplicate serial-number plates: my own and that of another robot that looked just like me. When I'd finished the job, I put the plates out of sight and began doing other things around the ship.

It wasn't as long a run as from Ganymede to Mars, but the *Terrabella* was slow, and I guess the time dragged for Captain Becker.

He seemed more restless than on the longer run, and played wilder, crazier music. Once in a while, when I passed his cabin or stopped off for something, he would look up and say, "That was recorded in the mountains of Pluto. It isn't instrumental. It's the voices of a primitive silicone tribe that eats ground rock."

I didn't say anything, but it sounded to me as though the rock was giving them stomach-aches at the time of the recording.

Or he would say, "That's the death chant of the savages

on Jupiter's third moon. They kill all the old men and women after they reach a certain age."

Once he got even more restless than usual and called for me. When I got to his cabin, he had an old book. It was bound in black leather. He handed it to me.

"You can read, can't you?"

"Yes."

"All right. Read me this book."

I took the book. On the cover it said, *Holy Bible*, and inside, on the page it was open to, were the words: The Old Testament. I wondered what that was.

"Read it," Captain Becker said.

" 'In the beginning God created the heaven and the earth.' "

"Do you know what that means?"

"No."

"It tells about the creation of the world."

"What is creation?"

"To create is to make."

"The world was made?"

"Yes.

"I supposed it was always here."

"No. In the beginning God made it, and in time it will pass away."

I wanted to ask who God was, but I went on reading because that was what he had ordered me to do.

After I'd read it for quite a while, he took it away from me and handed me another book. This one said *A Tale of Two Cities*, and it had been written by a human named Charles Dickens, probably an Earthman, I thought.

It started out very crazy: " 'It was the best of times, it was the worst of times . . .' "

I wanted to tell Captain Becker how silly that was. It couldn't have been both. It had to be one or the other. But Captain Becker didn't say anything. He seemed to accept what Mr. Dickens said, and I decided it was something Paul hadn't taught me.

I read from the book for quite a while, and then Captain Becker got tired of listening and reached for it.

"You read pretty well. Too bad you have to go back to an herb farm on Ganymede."

I went back to work wondering who God was and how it had been possible to make the world in six days.

As we moved in toward the Earth I began watching the skies more and more. All the stars and planets looked bigger here in the inner part of the System, and we could see Earth itself getting bigger and bigger all the time.

It was a blue color — very beautiful, I thought — and at times I could hardly take my refractor bulb off it.

It was the place where I'd been born. Of course I shouldn't have been able to remember anything about it, but somehow I did — or thought I did. It felt like home to me — a strange feeling I couldn't put into words. Ganymede seemed unreal — a far, far place I'd never been to. But a place I would have to go back to.

The blue planet. My home, and yet there was no place for me on it!

As we got closer, I could see the shapes I'd seen in the pictures in Paul's books. Continents, he'd called them, and I could even pick out the one called North America,

159

with the United States at the bottom of it. That was where I had been made. In the United States. And that was where we were going. But I didn't think much about those things. What I thought of was Paul.

Then, quite suddenly, when I was looking out into the sky during one of the watches, I knew what "ashamed" meant. Because that was how I felt.

Ashamed.

Maybe not that exactly, but as Paul would have said, what I felt would do until "ashamed" came along.

I went to Captain Becker's cabin and said, "Paul is on the *Oklahoma*. It's a luxury space liner that left Mars three days before we did. I think it will be reaching Earth in a few more days — ahead of us."

He didn't seem too surprised at what I told him. He looked at me thoughtfully and said, "Well, great galaxies! What brought that revelation out?"

"What is revelation?"

"Why are you telling me now?"

"Because I don't think Paul got in touch with his parents. I doubt if he remembered to let them know he was coming, and I'm sure they're very worried. I don't want them to worry any more."

"Do tell!"

I didn't know what that meant, but I didn't ask. I said, "I thought maybe you might send them a message. You could tell them Paul is on the way home."

"That would open a big line of inquiry."

"I don't understand."

"Wouldn't the authorities want to know how I came by the information?"

"You could tell them I told you."

"They would want to know how you knew."

"We were going to board the space liner together. I held back at the last minute because they would have stopped me. They have a rule that robots must go by freight."

He thought that over, and then said, "You're telling me Paul deserted you at Marspoint and went on home?"

"No. He thought I was following him on. When he found out I wasn't, it was too late. The port was locked. The jet-off countdown had started."

"I see."

"Will you send the message?"

"I can't rightly say. I'll have to think it over."

"They would stop worrying."

"It won't be much longer. If the *Oklahoma* started three days ahead of us, she's almost in by now."

"It would be nice if they knew."

He squinted at me. "I've been watching you. You've been spending a lot of time looking out into the void."

"It's very pretty. The stars are bigger."

"Earth's bigger too, isn't it?"

"Yes."

"Maybe you're getting a yen to set foot on it?"

"I'm going to Ganymede."

"That's right. You are. I meant it when I said you weren't going to leave the ship. I've had enough close calls in this little affair. In this day and age, Space Authority pulls a man's license and then talks it over. I could sit in berth for a year while the wheels were turning."

"What wheels?"

161

"Never mind. I just wanted to remind you that I'll be watching. Don't try any of your robot tricks."

I didn't say anything.

"That's all. Go find some work to do."

I left his cabin, and something else had changed. I wasn't thinking the same way any more. Maybe it was Earth coming closer and closer. Maybe it was because the thing Paul called "will power" just wasn't built into me.

Anyhow, with Earth hanging out there in the sky — where Paul was — I knew I was going to put my two feet on Earth. I was going to see Paul again or be destroyed trying.

I had changed my ideas.

And I felt better; now I'd made the decision, I didn't have to keep scratching around in my control box for ideas. There was no point in long-range planning. I didn't know what I would be up against.

I only knew I was going to hunt for Paul.

And I wasn't afraid. I felt wonderful.

16. Dead End

WE BERTHED IN KANSAS CITY seven days later.
A few hours before landing, I'd washed myself and the other three robots very carefully, taking special care with the one whose serial number I'd duplicated.

Just before coming in, I had taken that robot into the machine shop and tacked the duplicate of my serial number over his. When it was tightly in place, I'd sent him back to the cargo hold and tacked his duplicate over mine. With the change made, I waited for the landing and the unloading job Captain Becker would put us to work on.

He never paid any attention to serial numbers. The three robots looked alike to him, and I looked like any or all of them. The only way he knew me was that when he called my name I always came. The others paid no attention. We no longer used the strings on their arms.

163

As soon as we were in, he started all four of us unloading cargo immediately.

In loading and unloading, Captain Becker had gotten used to having me work the pile. That meant, in unloading, that I would stay in the hold and direct the order in which the crates were removed.

I did that for a while, going to the port once in a while to look out. It was funny to see Captain Becker standing out there in the open without his helmet. I kept expecting him to grab his throat and fall down from lack of air. But of course Earth has all the air humans need. But it was hard to get used to, seeing people roam around with nothing on but their clothes.

We unloaded all day and most of the next. Then, when the hold was almost empty, I changed places with the robot that was wearing my serial number.

It was easy to do this. I ordered the robot to work the rest of the cargo. I took his crate and carried it out of the hold, and came back in behind the other two robots.

Captain Becker didn't notice the change. I could tell by watching him that he thought I was still in the cargo hold.

That was what I wanted him to think.

Finally the hold was empty. He checked the pile outside and came up the ramp. I followed him with the other two robots, and when I got inside he'd already finished what he'd had in mind. He'd stood the robot he thought was me against a bulkhead and taken its batteries out.

"Sorry to do this, Rex," he said, "but it's for the best."

I agreed with him. I thought it was for the best too. He wouldn't be hunting for me after I left the ship, and he wouldn't be going into the hold for a while, so he wouldn't even know a robot was missing — not until the new cargo arrived.

Then he scared me. He turned away from the deactivated robot, paused for a second, and turned back. It looked as though he'd spotted the mistake.

He scowled at it for a moment, and across to where we were standing. And that was where the work I had done on the plates saved me. He bent over and checked the serial number on the deactivated robot.

When he grunted and straightened up, it was all right. He hadn't really been able to tell us apart, but something had bothered him.

This was where chance came in — something I hadn't been able to do anything about. I'd known from the beginning that my whole plan would be no good if Captain Becker decided to turn all the robots off. He might have decided to do that, because he did it on the Ganymede-Mars run when the robots were not in use, and for a little while on the last run.

Luckily he didn't do it now. That meant he expected the new cargo in a day or so and didn't think it worth while. After all, the charges didn't cost him anything, because he had his own generator.

It was a touchy moment, however, and I was thankful when he left the hold by way of the inner cargo port.

My plan had worked. At least, I had a fair chance to get away.

I waited there in the hold with my diaphragms tuned sharply. I could hear him moving around in the forward end of the ship.

Soon the pilot's port closed. I heard it lock and there was silence. He had left the ship.

I left the ship too. It was easy. He hadn't bothered to lock the inner cargo hold port, and I went forward and did exactly what he had done. I set the pilot's port timer on a two-minute relock and went out and down the ramp, leaving the ship all snug behind me.

At the end of the ramp I stopped and turned around and said good-bye to the *Terrabella*. Whatever happened, I doubted if I would ever see her again. She'd been a good ship. She'd brought us a long way through the void without complaint, and I felt good at having been able to do little things for her — repair her fin and clean her up inside.

Then I turned away and faced the future.

It was all very confusing. Earth was different. Too many people. Too many robots. Too much going on all the time. Beside the Kansas City spaceport, all others I'd ever seen looked like sleepy little way stations on the road to nowhere.

This helped a lot, because in all that activity nobody noticed me. I walked until I was quite a way from the spaceport, and then I stopped and stood motionless by a wall while I tried to figure out some plans.

First, I knew I had to get from Kansas City to Toledo. Paul had told me that there were two methods of transportation: copters and monorails. I didn't see how I could use either one, because I didn't have any money. I was going to have to find another way to get to Toledo.

I thought of the visiphone. I could call the Simpson

home collect and ask to talk to Paul. I'd never used a visiphone, but I didn't think it would be hard to figure out.

There were points that bothered me. First, maybe they wouldn't let me talk to Paul. I was pretty sure the *Oklahoma* had already berthed in Toledo and gone on to its other ports of call, and that Paul was home with his family.

But his father might answer and be angry, and alert the police in Kansas City. I decided I would have to take a chance on that.

The other thing I wondered about was whether robots were allowed to use visiphones. I checked that out by standing around and watching. I watched for an hour and saw quite a few domestics and other higher-type robots go into the visibooths. Evidently they were allowed to use the phones to call their owners and get instructions and such.

I went into a booth and looked the instrument over. As I said, it wasn't very complicated. There was a card on the wall telling exactly what to do. I picked up the receiver and dialed the way it said, and the operator's voice came in along with her face on the visiplate.

"I want to talk to Paul Simpson in Toledo," I said. "He will pay at that end."

"You wish to call person-to-person?"

"Yes."

"What is the number?"

"I don't know."

"What is the address of the Simpson residence?"

"I don't know."

The operator, a pretty Earthgirl, frowned. She evidently

thought that here was a robot that didn't know much of anything.

"I will look the number up if you can give me the name under which the phone would be listed."

"Paul's father's name is Roger Simpson."

"I'll look the number up for you."

Her face went off the screen, but she soon came back. She smiled. "I have the number. I will connect you."

I waited, hearing a lot of noises over the phone. Then there was a silence and the girl appeared in the visiplate again.

"I am sorry. That number has been disconnected."

"Do you mean the Simpsons don't live in Toledo?"

"There is a number listed under that name, but it was disconnected a very short time ago."

I didn't know exactly what all that meant, except that I wasn't going to talk to Paul in Toledo.

"I'm sorry," the girl said. The visiplate went blank, and the receiver croaked in my ear as though it were telling me to get off the line and quit holding things up. I put the receiver down and went out of the booth.

I didn't know what to do. How could I get in touch with Paul?

I went out into the street, not knowing what to do. Nobody paid any attention to me because there were so many robots moving around. I stood there a while and finally decided I had to ask some questions. There were things I had to find out. I couldn't ask humans, and there was only one thing left. I had to find a robot to talk to.

I began walking, putting all my attention on the robots I saw. Most of them were inferior types — errand robots carrying packages and making deliveries to addresses they'd been given.

I had to find a domestic with a high intelligence quota. I never found one, but I didn't have to. I began getting news and information through other sources.

This happened when I stopped beside the entrance to a busy store of some kind where they had a loudspeaker giving out the news.

As I stood there watching robots walk by, I heard the newscaster say:

"The *Oklahoma*, plush luxury space liner plying the inner spaceways, has just been released from long Lunar quarantine. A rare Martian disease was discovered when one of the passengers, a young girl, was stricken en route. The ship was held on Luna until checks and vaccinations eliminated all possibility of the disease virus reaching Earth. The *Oklahoma* berths at its first port of call, Kansas City, today."

That gave me a lot to think about. Paul had not yet reached Earth. The *Oklahoma* would berth at Kansas City before it went on to Toledo. First I had a flash of hope, but that died quickly. It would not put me any closer to Paul. He wouldn't get off the ship at Kansas City. He had no way of knowing I was there. He probably thought I had been destroyed or lost back on Mars. He would be very hurt, and probably wouldn't care what happened to me after my deserting him.

Then I thought of the other thing. His folks were not where he expected them to be. Maybe they weren't even in Toledo. He would get there and find no one to welcome him, and be as bad off as he'd been on Mars.

When I thought that over, I realized it wasn't true. Paul wasn't a fool. He knew the company his father now worked for. It was still in Toledo. He could ask about them and find out where they went.

No, Paul would be all right. The whole point was, would I ever find him?

The chances weren't very good.

While I was standing there thinking, I heard something else, something that made me very sad.

There was a lunch counter in the store where the newscast was coming from, and two humans at the counter were talking to each other. They were both males. One of them said, "That *Oklahoma*. She's a hard-luck ship."

The other one asked, "What do you mean?"

"Didn't you hear? They've got a kid aboard. A juvenile delinquent from Ganymede."

The other man said, "I hadn't heard, but can you imagine that? They've got juvenile delinquents all over the System, haven't they?"

"This one stole a valuable robot out there in one of the colonies. Right off some guy's farm. He smuggled it onto a freighter to Mars. He was trying to get it to Earth."

"What was his idea? What was he going to do with a robot?"

"I heard several stories on it. It got a lot of interest because it was the first time anything like that had ever happened. One story said the boy had ideas about starting a hijacking gang using only robots. Another had it that he was going to teach the robot to make speeches and start a robot revolution."

"Good heavens!"

"I think the kid was planning to sell the robot. He could have gotten a better price here on Earth than out in the System."

"What happened to the robot?"

"Nobody seems to know. It isn't on the ship with him. The story came from several sources — Ganymede, Mars, the *Oklahoma* en route. It will all be cleared up when the police get their hands on the kid. He's in real trouble. They'll probably make an example of him."

One of the men finished his coffee and left, but I'd heard enough. Paul was in bad trouble, and there was nothing I could do about it. He was going to be arrested for stealing me, and even though it wasn't true there would be no one to speak for him. No one except Captain Becker, and I was sure he would keep his mouth shut and get away from Earth as soon as possible. He didn't want to get mixed up in anything that might get him in trouble.

I knew the law was the law, and no matter how important Paul's father was he could not keep them from doing what the man said — making an example of his son.

Paul was probably already under arrest. I wondered whether they would put him off the ship at Kansas City or take him on to Toledo.

And Paul didn't even know where his father was!

I walked around, wondering what to do — how I could help Paul. I could go to the police station and tell the policemen that none of it was true, but that wouldn't help. A robot is not allowed to testify in court. If he does say anything, it is stricken from the record. The reason for this is that a robot is not a human; it doesn't have a soul, and therefore it cannot take an oath to tell the truth the way humans can.

I'd learned that from one of Paul's books, and I wondered about it. It's impossible for a robot to lie to a direct question. Why should it have to take an oath?

Paul couldn't answer that. "It's the way the law reads," he had said.

I started walking around the city so as not to look suspicious by standing in one place and doing nothing. I began to feel hungry and knew my charge was running out.

For a while I concentrated my whole thought on this, because I didn't want to go unconscious at this stage of things. I walked until I found a place where there were washrooms.

I went inside and stood around as though I was waiting for my master, and when the washroom was empty I ducked into one of the booths and locked the door.

Changing my own batteries was tricky, but I could do it. What I had to avoid was disconnecting the old ones, even for a second, before I got the new ones connected. If I did that, I would go unconscious and freeze. Then I would have to wait for a human to connect me up again.

I opened my torso box carefully and reached in and found the wires and the terminal posts. I connected the wires of the new battery, lowering my head so that I could get the cavity just within range of my refractor bulb.

When they were connected, I waited for an overcharge, but it didn't come. That meant my old batteries were so weak that the new ones didn't overcharge. All I had to do was disconnect the wires of the old batteries and take them out.

I put them on the floor and waited until it was quiet in the washroom and went back out into the street.

I began to walk again. I decided there was only one thing I could possibly do — something that probably wouldn't help a bit.

I turned and looked at the passing crowd. Then I walked over to a uniformed policeman who was walking by.

I hit him hard enough to knock him down.

I ran off, and the cry, "Mad robot! Mad robot!" rose up behind me.

17. Surrender

THE IDEA THAT HAD COME TO ME was pretty simple. I would go mad, and they would either melt me down with a ray gun or capture me. Either way, they would eventually find out I was the robot from Ganymede, and that first story — the one about my kidnaping Paul — would stand up under inquiry.

How else could they figure it when they had the mad robot to prove it? That was the idea, but my job was to make a big fuss so I would be noticed.

After knocking the policeman down I ran across the street and up the other side. Some people got in my way, but I didn't touch them. A berserk robot would have done this — knocked down anything or anybody who got in its way.

I managed to slow down a little and let people get out of the way. One female screamed and sprawled on the sidewalk right in front of me, but I jumped over her instead of trampling her.

The cry, "Mad robot!" was going up everywhere, and people were running in all directions. The robots didn't run. They either went right on about their business or turned to look at me.

I had to keep on running of course, because that's what a mad robot always does. If I'd stopped to let the police catch up with me, it wouldn't have made any sense.

So I kept on running and the people kept screaming and getting out of the way. I passed a lot of other robots, and then something happened that I couldn't understand. One of them — an intelligent-looking domestic — waved his arms and took out after me.

I'd never heard of a robot geared to chase other ones — to go after mad robots — but maybe this one was something new. Maybe they had manufactured some police robots with quotients for chasing criminals.

This didn't seem very likely, but there was one chasing me and waving its arms.

I heard police sirens around me in the various streets, but no organized squads of policemen got in my way or moved in on me.

I thought that my attack of "madness" had come so abruptly it had caught the police with their guards down. I kept on running, and the only chasing was being done by the crazy robot coming along behind me.

I didn't want to be taken by another of my own kind. I wanted humans to do it. Perhaps that was pride, and Paul had told me that pride wasn't a very good thing to have, that only certain kinds were good. I hoped this was the right kind, but still I wasn't going to let that robot catch me.

I turned into a narrow street, hoping the robot would miss me, but he didn't. He turned in after me, waving his arms and yelling without making any words.

I'd gone only a few feet when I found it was a dead-end street. It was a quiet place — nobody around except two children playing at the far end.

I didn't know what to do.

Suddenly I saw a way out — a door that was standing half open on one side near the far end. I ran in that direction, adding a few yells of my own to those of the other robot so that police would not lose track of us. I figured if I yelled they could find me more easily.

There were the sounds of patrol sirens all around and loudspeakers warning the people to stay out of the way. I realized the police hadn't really been slow at all.

They were closing in very fast, and soon it would be all over. But I was going to stay clear as long as I could. I didn't want to have my control box melted down until absolutely necessary. I headed for that doorway and was diving through it when I caught sight of the other robot through the outer edge of my refractor bulb.

He wasn't following me any more. He was going straight ahead toward the blind end of the street, and I realized what he was — a real mad robot.

He had probably been right on the edge of madness, and seeing me kick up such a fuss had tipped him over the line. He had followed me for a little while, probably without even realizing it.

Then his control box had gone all out and he began following the pattern of true madness — blind, driving movement in one direction until something stopped him.

When he hit the wall at the end of the street, he would smash through it if he could. Otherwise he would keep smashing against the wall until something gave — the wall or the robot.

I saw the rest of it, or rather I realized what the true situation was. Two small human children were playing against the wall right in the robot's path — kids too small and too scared to move. The robot would trample them to death.

I don't know why I didn't want this to happen. It shouldn't have occurred to a robot with my quotients, but it did. Without thinking, I turned back from the doorway and lunged back into the street to get between the robot and the children.

I made it in time to brace myself against the robot's charge. I wasn't able to get directly in front of him, but he slammed into me and went off at an angle without being knocked down. I staggered from the impact and my diaphragms rang like bells.

For a few minutes I lost my orientation and struggled to get it back. When my control box began working again, I saw two things. The robot had hit a side wall, staggered back in kind of a circle, and was heading for the dead end and the children again.

Also, the police had come. Uniformed human males were crowding into the other end of the street.

They had ray guns, and several of them were raised. One of the policemen, evidently the one in charge, yelled, "Don't shoot! You can't shoot! You'll kill a lot of people!"

He probably meant the two children. But there were a lot of other people hanging out of windows. They had been attracted by the racket and wanted to see what was going on.

I didn't pay much attention to any of that. The robot was headed for the wall, and the children were screaming.

This time I got in front of the robot. Completely mad, I doubt if he saw me or knew I was there. This gave me a little advantage because it let me brace myself, and the robot didn't put on any extra effort to knock me aside.

That was probably the difference. As it was, when he collided with me I felt as though a spaceship had rammed into me going a million miles an hour.

My refractor bulb lighted up like the picture of the Christmas tree I'd seen in one of Captain Becker's books. My diaphragms sounded as though someone had smashed a rock mountain with a big sledge hammer.

I pivoted in a circle and went staggering away, trying to hold my balance. I was just able to, and when my tube cleared, I saw that the other robot had gone down and was struggling helplessly on the ground.

It couldn't hurt the kids, but the police were pouring in, and it was too late for me to find the open door and run.

It was the end. They could come close and use their ray guns and not be afraid of hitting anybody.

They came in fast, a line of them, and their guns came up against their shoulders.

I backed against the wall and waited.

I knew the gunners' trigger fingers were tightening, and I had time for one thought: how would it feel to have my control box destroyed?

Then the leader threw up his hands and yelled, "Wait a minute! Don't shoot."

They looked at him as though they thought he'd gone out of his mind, and one of them yelled, "Sergeant! It'll charge any second! Give us a break!"

The sergeant — I'd been watching him — had been looking at the cowering children and the downed robot with a kind of questioning expression.

He said, "There's something funny here. This other robot —"

One of the men lowered his gun. "It's pretty obvious, Sergeant. Both robots went crazy. The kids were lucky. The one still standing stumbled in the way of the other and knocked him down."

"I'm not so sure."

"I'll fry this one and we'll check afterward."

That was logical. It was the way humans always handled mad robots. The only safe way.

But the sergeant was looking at me with his eyes narrowed. He waved a restraining hand at the men and moved slowly forward.

"Watch it, Sergeant!" one of the men cried. "He's going to charge!"

The sergeant paid no attention. He came slowly toward me.

I yelled, "I'm a mad robot! Look out!"

"Sure you are," the sergeant said, but there was a low, soothing note in his voice.

"I'm very mad. I ran and knocked down everything in my way!"

"Sure you did."

179

"I came from Ganymede. Robots get very mad out there."

"Very mad." He kept coming closer.

"I worked on a farm out there, and kidnaped a boy."

"Uh-huh."

"I put this boy on a spaceship on Mars and sent him to Earth."

"How did you get to Earth?"

"I came on a freighter. I'm a very mean robot, besides being mad. I ran away, and beat the captain playing chess, and changed my serial number."

"You've been awfully busy," the sergeant said.

"I'm going to charge you."

"Sure you are."

"Look out, Sergeant!" one of the men yelled. "He means it. I'm going to stop him."

The sergeant waved his hand behind him while keeping his eyes on me. "Put that gun down. I'll tell you when to use it."

He'd stopped now, and I knew I was going to have to charge him. I got set, but then he asked, "This boy you kidnaped. How did you get him from Ganymede to Mars?"

I had to answer his question before I charged, of course, because a robot is always supposed to answer anything a human asks.

"On the same freighter. I put him aboard in a cargo crate," I said.

"How about the captain? Didn't he object?"

"He didn't know anything about it."

"What were you going to do with the boy when you got him to Earth?"

"I was going to sell him in order to start a revolution."

I knew I'd gotten something mixed up in my memory bank on that one, but I thought the sergeant might not notice.

But he did. "It has to be the other way around," he said. "The boy could sell you, but you couldn't sell the boy."

That meant I wasn't getting anywhere. It meant he still believed Paul had stolen me.

"No! No!" I yelled. "I kidnaped the boy. That's how it was."

He was still coming forward very slowly. His eyes stared at my refractor bulb as though he were trying to read something there.

All the people were looking out of the windows, and everybody was very quiet. One of the gunners moaned, "Watch it, Sergeant! Watch it! You're getting too close! It'll get its arms on you and smash you."

The sergeant was a tall man. He looked a little like Mr. Simpson, Paul's father. He had the same kind of firm, kindly face.

One of the children that the other robot had almost smashed got up from where he'd been playing and started toward me. He didn't seem to be afraid. He was full of curiosity.

A woman watching let out a frightened squall and tumbled out of a window and rushed toward the child. She carried him back out of the way.

The sergeant paid no attention to any of this. He kept coming closer and closer.

"So you kidnaped a boy on Ganymede and brought him clear to Earth. Was that it?"

181

"Yes. That proves I'm a mad robot. That was why I did it."

The sergeant put his hands out, reaching for the door to my control box.

I said, "That serial number isn't mine. I made it and tacked it over my own so I could get away. But you're too smart for me. You've caught the mad robot, and now Paul can go home to his father and mother."

"Sure he can," the sergeant said.

He opened the door on the front of my torso box and reached inside. I realized I'd failed. He hadn't believed me. He hadn't believed a word I'd said. He had kept talking so he could get close enough to deactivate me.

I tried to charge, but I was too late. He snapped the switch, and it was the end of me.

But not quite the end. As my batteries stopped delivering, I had a dream. I was way out in space — out among the stars riding outside the hull of the *Terrabella*, and it was dark all around me, but I could still see.

I could see all the worlds, on and on, into infinity. I thought how lucky humans were to have all that space to travel, all those worlds to visit, all those strange people to meet and help and get to know.

It must be wonderful to be human, I thought.

All in a microsecond.

Then there was nothing . . .

18. Resurrection

I WAS CONSCIOUS.

I knew that first. My reflector bulb caught and my diaphragms buzzed, and I could see and hear.

I was standing in a room that turned out to be a part of the police station. The sergeant who had deactivated me was there.

But I hardly saw him because of the others. Paul was there. Captain Becker was there. Mr. Simpson. Even Jane, Paul's sister, with her hand on my arm and a smile that told me she was very glad to see me.

They were all smiling, and everybody understood.

Except me. I didn't understand anything.

Paul laughed when he saw my bulb light up. "Rex! You're all right again. Everything is all right."

"How can it be all right?" I asked. "I was deactivated. I failed."

"You didn't fool the sergeant with your act. He saw you go out of your way to save those kids."

"I don't understand. I don't understand any of it."

"You're a free robot, Rex," Mr. Simpson said. "The first one in history." He handed me a paper. I took the paper, but I didn't read it.

"And you're famous too, Rex!" Paul cried. "The most famous robot in the world. The Glenwood Laboratories want you to go through some research tests. To help them make better robots in the future."

"But what happened? Things can't be this way. I must be dreaming."

There were two other men in the room. One looked at the other with excitement. "Did you hear that? Doubt! Imagination! Where does it come from? How was it achieved?"

"This is Rex, gentlemen," Paul laughed. "You must not be surprised at anything he does. He's a very special robot."

"He certainly is," the other man said.

"They're from Glenwood, Rex," Paul told me. "They're the men who want to make the scientific tests."

"A robot that can simulate madness," one of them said. "Incredible!"

The police sergeant laughed. "He didn't do a very good job of it."

The man scowled. "You don't understand. He had the concept. The ability to try."

"He had that all right."

Captain Becker pushed forward. "I'll never live this down. A robot tying me up in knots on my own ship. Counterfeiting his serial number!"

I didn't know what some of those words meant, but I didn't care because Captain Becker wasn't mad. He was grinning.

"What are you and your father doing here, Paul?" I asked.

"Captain Becker sent Dad a radiogram from out on the spaceways, so he wouldn't worry. When Dad got it, he came to Kansas City and was waiting for me when the *Oklahoma* was released from quarantine."

"Young scalawag," Mr. Simpson growled. "Causing your mother and me all that worry. There'll be a few penalties for you, young man."

"Yes, Dad," Paul said quietly, "I've got them coming. But may I answer Rex's questions?"

"Certainly. He deserves answers."

"Your family had moved, Paul. How did the radiogram get through?"

"It was forwarded, Rex," Mr. Simpson said. "We went into temporary quarters when we reached Toledo, and when we got our permanent home the number was changed. But the Kansas City operator hadn't received it yet."

"You know about that too?"

The sergeant smiled. "When we start digging into a case, we're pretty thorough," he said.

The two men kept looking at each other and shaking

their heads and muttering, "Incredible. Remarkable."

"This may be a definite breakthrough in the field," one of them said.

"What about Mr. Hennings? I belong to him. Won't he want me back?" I dreaded to ask this question.

"It's been ascertained that no theft occurred," Captain Becker said. "Technically, you're a runaway, and Paul is involved — "

"Aiding and abetting the runaway," Mr. Simpson said sternly.

Paul said nothing. He hung onto the arm Jane wasn't holding and began scratching some dirt off my torso box.

"But all charges have been dropped," the police sergeant said.

"And the Glenwood people, not wanting you to get off Earth, paid Mr. Hennings so much money for you that he couldn't afford to turn them down."

"They've bought me?" I asked, looking at the paper in my hand.

One of the Glenwood men shook his head. "No. We have freed you. It's a part of a big new public-relations campaign one of our bright young men thought up. Build public confidence in robots. Make people realize the untapped potential of the whole field. You're going to be the father of an entire new Glenwood line, Rex."

"That is, if we can find out what makes you tick," the other man said with a smile.

"But what will I do? Where will I go? Only humans can have homes of their own, and families."

"Where do you want to go, Rex?" Captain Becker asked the question. "Out on the spaceways and play chess with me?" He grinned.

"That won't be possible, I'm afraid," the Glenwood man said. "Rex will be very busy here on Earth. He'll do a lot of traveling — meet a lot of people."

"And there will be the tests," the other one said.

I looked at Paul. "We won't be — "

"We will too!" he cried. "Your home will be with us. It's where you belong. You'll travel a lot, but you'll always come home."

Home! Home on Earth! The thought made my control box tickle.

Still looking at Paul, I said, "I just thought of something."

"What, Rex?"

"I didn't do anything. I didn't help you a bit."

"What do you mean?"

"Remarkable," the Glenwood man muttered.

"I mean if I'd done nothing at all, everything would have worked out for you. All that talk I overheard about your stealing me and how serious it was for you were only rumors."

"You'll have to learn that about humans, Rex," the police sergeant said. "They say a lot of irresponsible things. They aren't as reliable as robots."

"You did do something for me, Rex," Paul said.

"What did I do?"

"You made me the proudest boy on Earth, that's what.

187

Not only that, but I'm famous too — as the boy who owned Rex, the great robot."

"I'm very glad," I said.

"Remarkable," the Glenwood man said.

I decided to agree with him, at least until I found out what all those words meant. But at that moment I was too happy to care.